DOCTOR WHO

The Blood Cell

JAMES GOSS

ISBN 978-0-8041-4092-8

'Release the Doctor – or the killing will start.'

An asteroid in the furthest reaches of space – the most secure prison for the most dangerous of criminals. The Governor is responsible for the cruellest murderers. So he's not impressed by the arrival of the man they're calling the most dangerous criminal in the quadrant. Or, as he prefers to be known, the Doctor.

But when the new prisoner immediately sets about trying to escape, and keeps trying, the Governor sets out to find out why.

Who is the Doctor and what's he really doing here? And who is the young woman who comes every day to visit him, only to be turned away by the guards?

When the killing finally starts, the Governor begins to get his answers…

An original novel featuring the Twelfth Doctor and Clara, as played by Peter Capaldi and Jenna Coleman

BBC DOCTOR WHO

The Crawling Terror

BBC

DOCTOR WHO

The Crawling Terror

Mike Tucker

B\D\W\Y
Broadway Books
New York

Copyright © 2014 by Mike Tucker

All rights reserved.
Published in the United States by Broadway Books, an imprint
of the Crown Publishing Group, a division of Random House LLC,
a Penguin Random House Company, New York.
www.crownpublishing.com

Broadway Books and its logo, B\D\W\Y, are trademarks of Random House LLC.

This edition published by arrangement with
BBC Books, an imprint of Ebury Publishing,
a division of the Random House Group Ltd.

Doctor Who is a BBC Wales production for BBC One. Executive
producers: Steven Moffat and Caroline Skinner.

BBC, DOCTOR WHO, and TARDIS (word marks, logos, and devices)
are trademarks of the British Broadcasting Corporation and are used
under license.

Library of Congress Cataloging-in-Publication Data is available upon request

ISBN 978-0-8041-4090-4
eBook ISBN 978-0-8041-4091-1

Printed in the United States of America

Editorial director: Albert DePetrillo
Series consultant: Justin Richards
Project editor: Steve Tribe
Cover design: Lee Binding © Woodlands Books Ltd 2014
Production: Alex Goddard

10 9 8 7 6 5 4 3 2 1

First U.S. Edition

For Karen

Prologue

Gabby Nichols gave a deep sigh of relief. She had been starting to think that Wayne was never going to stop crying. Watching him now, curled up in the blankets of his cot, silent and content, it was difficult to believe that this was the same red-faced, screaming baby that she had been carrying around the house for the last hour.

Not for the first time that evening, Gabby wished that her husband were here. Wayne always seemed to go to sleep more quickly in the arms of his father. Roy Nichols was part of the team building the new high-speed rail link between London and the South West. It had meant relocating from their house in Manchester and renting one down here in Wiltshire, but it was a seven-year contract, and it paid well. The downside was that Roy was doing a lot of shift work. Gabby had barely seen him over the last three nights.

She gave another sigh. At least he was going to be back at the weekend. In the meantime she had promised herself that as soon as Wayne was asleep she was going to treat herself to a couple of hours in front of the TV with the DVD box set of *Call the Midwife* and a glass of wine.

Turning on the baby monitor, she closed the door to Wayne's room and started to make her way downstairs. As on every other night that she had been here alone, Gabby was struck by how utterly silent their new house was. She had been brought up in Manchester, and had lived in cities all her life. She was used to the constant background hum of traffic and aircraft, and the constant yellow glow of streetlights. Here the silence was total and the nights… Gabby had never know such a complete darkness, or seen so many stars in the night sky.

As her thoughts drifted back to the house that she had left behind, Gabby felt the same pang of uncertainty that had plagued her ever since they had arrived in Ringstone. It wasn't that they hadn't been made welcome. On the contrary, the villagers had gone out of their way to make them feel at home. Their cottage on the edge of the village green was huge compared to their old house, and the children were going to be able to grow up in clean air and beautiful surroundings. Her daughter, Emily, was already starting to drop unsubtle hints about wanting a pony.

It was just… a feeling, a sense of unease that Gabby found herself unable to escape.

She shook her head, telling herself not to be stupid. It was just going to take her time to get used to a new home and a new routine, that was all. When Roy got back at the weekend they would go out, explore the area a bit. Try and get to know some of the neighbours.

Taking a clean wine glass from the dishwasher, Gabby opened the fridge and poured herself a large glass of Pinot Grigio. As she was raising the glass to her lips a shrill voice rang out from upstairs.

'Mummy!'

Gabby gave a groan of despair. Her daughter was 3, and prone to being very loud if she wanted attention. If she woke up Wayne…

'Mummy! Come quickly!'

Gabby frowned. There was a note of panic in her daughter's voice. Placing her wine glass down on the kitchen table, she hurried up the stairs.

'Emily?' She pushed open the door to her daughter's room. 'What is it, baby? Are you all right?'

Emily was pressed tight against the wall. Her eyes were wide with fear. She ran to her mother, hugging against her legs.

Gabby felt a jolt of panic. She had never seen her daughter so frightened. She lifted Emily into her arms. 'What's wrong?'

Emily had her face buried in her mother's shoulder. 'There's a huge daddy longlegs in my room.'

Gabby almost sobbed in relief, angry with herself for becoming so spooked. 'You're going to have to get used to that, sweetie.' She stroked her daughter's hair. 'We're in the countryside now. There's lots of insects here.'

'It's over there! It came through the window.'

Emily was still tucked tight against her. From the other side of the room Gabby could hear the paper-like rustling of the insect as it fluttered against the glass behind the curtains.

'Well, I'll just get rid of it and then we can get you back into bed.'

Gabby pulled the curtains back from the window and the breath caught in her throat as she caught sight of what was there.

Then she started to scream.

Alan Travers drained the last mouthful of his pint and shrugged into his heavy jacket. It was nearly the first day of spring but there was still a chill in the air at night and he had a long walk home.

'Sure you'll not stay for another, Alan?'

The tiny public bar of the Wheatsheaf was busy with its usual weekday mix of locals and tourists. Brian Cartwright was at the bar, a £20 note in his hand.

Alan shook his head. 'As unusual as it is to see you buying a round, I'm afraid I'm going to pass. I've got an early start in the morning, even if you layabouts don't. I'll see you gentlemen tomorrow.'

Pulling on his hat, Alan threaded his way through the jostling drinkers towards the door.

'Well you just be careful cutting through that science park!' Brian called after him. 'You know they're breeding monsters in there!'

As the door swung shut behind him, Alan could hear

laughter ring out through the pub. That joke had been a regular one ever since the park had been built of the edge of the village. Alan gave a snort of derision. Bio-fuels and GM crops. As far as he was concerned that *was* almost the same as breeding monsters.

Pulling up the collar of his jacket, he set off through the pub car park towards the industrial estate. It was a clear night, and a distant moon was casting a pale glow across the fields. Alan shivered. He should have had a coffee instead of that last beer. He lived in the next village over, and even cutting through the science park it was a good twenty-minute walk to get home.

The footpath around the village was accessed by a stile in the corner of the car park. He clambered over it unsteadily, almost losing his balance as he landed on the well-trodden path on the other side. He definitely shouldn't have had that final pint. He breathed in deeply, taking in a good lungful of the cool night air, then set off along the path.

As he approached the underpass that cut beneath the railway line, a tall shape suddenly loomed up from the darkness, making him start. With a barking laugh he realised that he'd been startled by one of the standing stones that formed the circle in the field close to the pub. In the moonlight the monolith could almost have been a hunched figure. Alan walked over to it, running his fingers over the swirls and patterns carved into the ancient rock.

Alan had always liked the stones. He liked that they

were a reminder of the natural world, not the clean, clinical science that dominated modern life. It had been the stones that had nearly scuppered the plans for the science park altogether. When the plans had first been published, there had been a huge public outcry at the desecration of an ancient site. Even though no burial ground had ever been found associated with the stones, public pressure had forced the development of the park to be moved to the other side of the railway line.

Alan couldn't understand why Ringstone had been chosen as a site for the park anyway. It wasn't exactly convenient. That in turn had started all the rumours about it concealing something untoward. That, and the fact that the businessman behind it had some kind of facial disfigurement. Poor beggar had to wear some kind of plastic surgical mask.

Patting the stone with approval, Alan set off along the path towards the underpass. Clouds had started to crawl across the face of the moon and Alan was beginning to regret not bringing a torch.

As he entered the tunnel, something brushed his face. With a cry Alan swiped at it with his hand, then immediately berated himself for being so jumpy. It was just a spider's web.

He wiped his hand on his jacket. The stuff was sticky, and strong. As he tried to brush off the strands, his arm caught in more of it. He pulled, but his arm was caught fast. He tugged hard at the web. He could barely break it.

Alan heaved with all his strength. There was a tearing

noise and the stitching on his jacket ripped at the sleeve. Suddenly free of the sticky grip, Alan lost his footing and stumbled backwards, falling into something soft and clinging. It was yet more of the web, great clumps of it clinging to the wall and ceiling of the underpass. Alarmed now, he tried to get back onto his feet, but the web held him fast. Alan started to panic, but the more he struggled to free himself the more of the strands tangled around him.

A sudden scrape from the end of the tunnel made him start. A shadow flickered across the far entrance.

'Is someone there?' Alan called out. 'I could do with some help!'

To his annoyance there was no reply, just the rustle of something brushing through the undergrowth.

'Come on, I'm not mucking about, I'm stuck here!'

The shadow started to move towards him, but as it came closer Alan realised with a sudden chill that the shape casting it was not remotely human. He became aware of a low rasping breathing, and the scratch of something harsh and bristly against the tiled walls of the underpass. The shape filled the tunnel.

As the patchy moonlight revealed what it was that had found him, Alan felt his heart give out.

Kevin Alperton woke with a jolt. For several moments he lay there in the dark, listening to the familiar sounds of the house, trying to determine what had woken him. He had been dreaming about ice cream. He'd been on a nice warm beach, with no school to think about, no teachers pestering him, nothing but sand and the distant swoosh of the sea on pebbles. That soothing noise had turned into something harsh and piercing, cutting into his dream and bringing him back to reality with a start.

He glanced over at his clock. It was gone eleven. Chances were that his parents were still up. It must have been them moving around downstairs that had woken him.

As he rolled over and tried to get himself comfortable again, a horrible howling shriek cut through the silence. The noise was like a cross between a wailing cat and a crying baby. It made the hairs on the back of Kevin's neck stand on end.

He groaned.

Foxes.

Every spring it was the same. As soon as it got dark and the roads were free of people then the latest batch of fox cubs came out to explore. When they were youngsters they were quite cute, but as soon as they got older they were a menace; pulling over bins, rummaging through compost piles and keeping half the village awake with their incessant howling.

Kevin buried his head in the pillow as the piercing sound rang out again, but he knew that it was pointless. Once they started, they would only stop if he scared them away.

Yawning, Kevin threw back his *Godzilla* duvet and hauled himself out of bed. After the sleepless nights that he had put up with last summer he had taken to leaving a 'Super Soaker' water pistol on his bedroom windowsill. He had wanted to use his catapult but his mum had told him that was cruel and dangerous and confiscated it.

As he neared the window, the howling cry came again, but this time there was something about the pitch, the level of the sound, that made Kevin's blood run cold. This wasn't the usual noise that he had heard before. This was a sound of pure primal fear and pain.

Nervously, Kevin pulled back the curtains and peered out of his bedroom window. The cloud-shrouded moon had turned the back garden into a patchwork of shadows, but in the centre of the lawn Kevin could just make out a writhing shape. It was a fox all right, but there seemed to be something wrong with it. Kevin pressed his nose to the glass, straining to see clearly. The fox seemed to be rolling on the scrubby grass, snapping and biting at its fur, whining and growling as it did so.

As Kevin tried to work out what on earth was going on, the moon suddenly emerged into a patch of clear sky and milky white light illuminated dozens of hard black shapes swarming over the stricken fox.

As Kevin jumped back from the window in alarm, there was a final desperate howl from outside, and then silence descended once more.

Kevin stood in the dark quiet of his room for a moment, unsure as to what he had just witnessed, and not sure if he wanted to look again. For a second he wondered if he should go downstairs and tell his parents what he had seen, but the thought of the withering look that he knew his father would give him made him think better of it.

Clambering back into his bed, Kevin tried to put the terrible sounds out of his head, but when he finally did get back to sleep, his dreams were no longer of ice cream and beaches, but of glistening black shapes, and terrible, doomed cries.

Chapter

One

The fields surrounding Ringstone were wreathed with mist as the morning sun slowly started to inch its way above the crow-filled trees. Abruptly, the chattering birds were sent spiralling into the air, cawing in annoyance as a grating, grinding rasp shattered the peace of the English countryside, and the bulky, blue shape of the TARDIS slowly faded into existence.

The instant it had fully materialised, the door was snatched open and the Doctor poked his head out into the morning air. In this incarnation the Doctor was a tall, thin-faced man with a tousled mop of silver-grey hair and intense eyes framed by unruly, expressive eyebrows.

Satisfied that he was in the right place, he stepped from the TARDIS, allowing a young, elfin-faced woman to follow him out.

'Where's this then?' asked Clara, looked around with mistrust. 'Distant past? Far-flung future? Alien planet that just happens to look like the English countryside?'

The Doctor glared at her. 'Wiltshire.'

'Wiltshire?' Clara gave him a nod of mock approval. 'You really *are* showing me the exotic corners of the universe.'

'Not entirely my choice,' said the Doctor turning slowly around on the spot as he tried to get his bearings. 'The TARDIS picked up some ley-line disturbance. Not much, but enough to warrant a brief investigation.'

'Ley lines?' Clara stared at him in disbelief. 'Please don't tell me that you've regenerated into a hippie.'

'I'll have you know that my tambourine solo was one of the highlights of Woodstock. Ah, There we are…' The Doctor was squinting through the clearing mist at a distant church spire. 'So, that should mean…' He traced an imaginary line in the air from the spire to the TARDIS then onwards to the far side of the field. 'This way.'

He set off through the mist, arm held out in front of him like some suited and booted scarecrow. With a sigh of weary resignation Clara pulled the TARDIS door shut and set off after him.

As soon as it was light, Kevin hurried downstairs and, pulling wellingtons on over his pyjamas, unlocked the back door and cautiously made his way over to where he had seen the fox.

Secretly he was hoping that there would be nothing to see, that he could dismiss what he had caught a glimpse of last night as nothing more than the result of an overactive imagination, but as he approached the end of the garden he could see a bundle of reddish-brown fur lying in the flowerbed.

Nervously, Kevin approached the remains of the dead fox. It looked strange – shrunken somehow. Picking up a discarded bamboo cane from his dad's vegetable patch, he prodded at the corpse. As he did so the fox seemed to collapse in on itself. To Kevin's horror he realised that there was nothing left of the flesh of the animal; it had all been eaten away by something. All that was left was skin and bone, a shell.

As Kevin knelt down to get a closer look, something rustled in the shrubbery, and he caught a glimpse of something black and shiny scuttling along the bottom of the fence that bordered next door's garden. Gripping his stick, Kevin pushed aside the branches, trying to get a better look at whatever the creature was.

With a sudden burst of speed, it vanished into a burrow in the earth. Kevin poked his stick into the hole. It was about the size of a rabbit burrow, but whatever had made this was no rabbit. In the darkness of the earth Kevin was certain he could see shapes moving. Wet, black shapes.

He leaned forward.

'Kevin?'

He jumped as his mum's voice rang out from the kitchen doorway. 'What are you doing out there in your pyjamas? You're going to be late for school again. Get back inside this instant!'

'I'm coming.' With a final poke into the hole, Kevin abandoned the bamboo cane and hurried back indoors.

As the door slammed shut something black and shiny

poked its head from the burrow, long antennae twitching in the morning air.

Clara wandered along the well-worn footpath through the field, enjoying the quiet stillness that was peculiar to early morning in the English countryside. It was rare that she had the opportunity to enjoy such moments of calm. Life with the Doctor – and life with the pupils of Coal Hill School for that matter – tended to be a lot more frantic.

She stopped, closing her eyes for a moment, listening to the hum of bees in the wild flowers, the cawing of the circling crows and the distant drone of a tractor. Shoreditch was never this tranquil. She wondered if Danny Pink would like the countryside. He didn't strike her as a country boy, but then Danny was always surprising her. Perhaps when she got back she should suggest a trip out somewhere, do a nice walk, and find a pub garden to have lunch in.

Aware that she was starting to daydream, Clara set off along the path once more. When she finally caught up with the Doctor, he was squatting in the centre of a wide circle of standing stones, peering at readings on his sonic screwdriver.

There were about a dozen or so of the stones, some no more than stubs of rock, others taller than she was. Each of them was inscribed with swirling, Celtic-looking patterns, the grooves in the stone worn shallow from hundreds of years of British weather.

'OK,' she muttered to herself. 'Ley lines it is, then.'

The Doctor had risen to his feet and was using his sonic screwdriver to scan the air above his head.

'What are you doing?'

'Checking to see whether there's a trapped spacecraft hovering in the hyperspatial dimension above the circle or not.'

'And… that happens a lot does it?'

'More often than you might think. But not this time.' He snapped the screwdriver closed and slipped it into his jacket pocket. 'This was the source of the energy reading that the TARDIS picked up, all right.' He waved an arm expansively around the circle. 'But the old girl has got her timing out a bit. This is totally dormant. Has been for years.'

'And you can tell that because…?'

'One of the stones is missing.' The Doctor pointed to where a stumpy bollard plugged a gap in the circle.

There was a small plaque bolted to the concrete with a short history of the site. Clara wandered over to it and started to read: 'The King's Guards is a Bronze Age monument located within the boundary of Ringstone Village in Wiltshire. Whilst its exact purpose remains unknown, the most likely explanation is that the stones form some kind of astrological calendar. The circle was damaged during a German bombing raid during the Second World War.'

Clara frowned. 'What on earth would the Germans be doing bombing a sleepy Wiltshire village?'

The Doctor's expression darkened. 'When did the

armed forces ever need a good reason to bomb anything?'

Clara mentally kicked herself. Since his regeneration, the Doctor had become decidedly prickly in his dealings with anything remotely military. That in itself might not have been a problem if it wasn't for the fact that her new boyfriend – her *potential* new boyfriend – was an ex-soldier.

She changed the subject. 'So, are we going to wander into the village? See if we can find somewhere to get some breakfast?'

'You go ahead; I'd like to see if I can work out what the real purpose of this circle was. If I can just recreate whatever pictogram was on this missing stone...'

The Doctor rummaged in his pocket and pulled out a stub of chalk. With quick, deliberate strokes he started drawing swirling Celtic patterns onto the concrete bollard.

'That's vandalism,' said Clara sternly.

The Doctor just glared at her.

'Suit yourself.' Clara shrugged. 'But don't blame me if you get locked up by the local police.'

'Then I shall rely on you to give me an exemplary character reference.' The Doctor started to dart from stone to stone, peering at the different symbols for a moment, then returning to his bollard, scrubbing out some chalk lines with his sleeve and adding new ones in their place.

Clara opened her mouth to retort that providing a character reference for a man who had recently changed his entire character might prove to be a little tricky, but then thought better of it. She was still getting used to this version of the Doctor. She had always known where she stood with *her* Doctor, always knew the boundaries of their relationship. This new one, however…

It was just going to take a bit of time, that was all.

Leaving the Doctor to his scribbling, Clara set off along the path towards the village.

Kevin checked his watch anxiously. He had now been waiting at the village bus stop for nearly twenty minutes. He was going to be late for school. Again.

It wasn't fair. It wasn't as though it was his fault this time. He had arrived at the bus stop with plenty of time to spare; the bus just hadn't turned up. Not that his teachers or his parents would be interested in hearing any excuses. It had been made quite plain that they wouldn't tolerate him being late again, no matter what the reason was.

The school was a good fifteen-minute walk away. If he set off now, he might just make it in time and save himself yet another evening of detention.

Kevin took one final look down the road to ensure that the bus wasn't coming. It would be just his luck for it to arrive just as he had decided to walk.

It suddenly struck Kevin that he hadn't seen *any* traffic on the road whatsoever. You couldn't exactly describe Ringstone as having a rush hour as such, but there was usually *some* traffic.

Kevin shrugged. Perhaps there had been an accident.

There were always lambs in the road at this time of year. The young ones didn't seem to have any road sense, and it was common for cars swerving to avoid them to end up in a ditch somewhere.

Consoling himself with the thought that if the road through the village was blocked then some of the other kids might be late as well, Kevin set off at a brisk pace. As he walked, he found himself thinking back to the remains of the fox that he had found in the garden. It was horrible. It had to have something to do with the black shape that he had seen in the burrow. He was certain that it had been an insect of some kind, but it was huge. Kevin was certain that there were no insects that big native to Britain.

A low, droning noise made him look up in alarm. Surely that wasn't the bus? As he did, something large buzzed past his head, making him duck. Kevin spun around to see what it was that had almost collided with him.

His eyes opened wide in astonishment. Sitting on a fencepost was a mosquito. But it was vast! It was easily as big as his hand. The creature tipped its head on one side, compound eyes regarding Kevin coldly, wings twitching. Fascinated and repulsed in equal measure, Kevin edged forward to get a closer look. As he did so, the huge insect launched itself into the air, its wings thrumming noisily.

Kevin stumbled backwards, swiping out in panic as the creature flew straight at him. He felt his hand connect with the spindly body and it crashed down onto the tarmac in an untidy tangle of legs.

Heart hammering in his chest, Kevin started to back away. The insect writhed on the roadway, trying to right itself. He looked around frantically for something to defend himself with. A flash of colour in the hedgerow caught his eye. It was a garish floral umbrella, probably discarded during the recent storm. Kevin grabbed the handle, struggling to pull it free. The metal ribs were bent and twisted, catching in the tightly-packed branches.

From behind him he could hear the deep bass humming of the mosquito's wings as it took flight once more. Not daring to look around Kevin pulled at the umbrella with all his might until, with a rip of fabric, it tore free.

Screaming with fear, Kevin spun around, lashing out with the improvised weapon. The mosquito was right behind him. Insect and umbrella collided with a sickening crunch. Caught up in the flapping fabric, the struggling insect wrenched the umbrella from Kevin's hand, and the entire tangled mess crashed to the ground.

Kevin didn't hesitate. Running forward, he stamped on the heaving, fluttering lump that thrashed under the fabric until the terrifying buzzing finally stopped.

Breathless and shaking, he stood back as thick yellow liquid started to ooze from under the brightly patterned umbrella. Then, from the fields around him, came more of the terrible noise, and half a dozen spindly shapes started to rise from the long grass.

Kevin turned and fled.

*

Clara followed the path from the stone circle along the side of a railway embankment. A wooden footpath sign indicated 'Ringstone Village Centre' in one direction, and 'Wyndham 3 miles' in the other. She was about to make her way down into the village when she caught sight of an underpass along the path in the other direction. There seemed to be something hanging just inside the entranceway. It looked like something wrapped in a sheet.

Puzzled, Clara started towards it. As she got closer she realised with a sudden chill that she had been horribly mistaken. It wasn't a sheet that billowed around the entrance of the tunnel. It was a web.

And there was a body in it.

Chapter

Two

Veterinary Surgeon Angela Drabble was just unlocking the door to her practice when she heard her name being called out and the sound of a baby crying.

She turned to see Gabby Nichols hurrying across the village green. She had her son in one arm, and something bundled up in a teacloth in the other. Her daughter was following along behind, dragging her feet and wearing the petulant pout that all 3-year-olds seemed to have when being asked to do something that they'd rather not do.

'Morning, Gabby.' Angela looked at the bundled teacloth. 'Not another injured blackbird, is it?'

'Not this time, Ang. I didn't know where else to bring it.'

Angela could see that Gabby was flustered and scared. She frowned. That wasn't like her. In the short time that Angela had known Gabby, she had struck her as being a very together young woman, one not easily panicked.

'Well, you'd better come inside and show me what

you've got.' Taking the bundle from her, Angela ushered Gabby and Emily into the surgery.

Once inside, she placed the bundle down on one of the examination tables and spent the next few minutes making sure that Emily was suitably entertained with a *Shaun the Sheep* book and a mug of squash. There were always kids in the surgery insisting that they had to stay near their pets, and Angela always made sure that she had plenty of material to distract them.

Leaving Emily in the waiting room, Angela closed the door to the examination room and started to unwrap the teacloth.

'Now, let's see what we have…'

As the last flap of fabric fell away she gave a sharp intake of breath.

'Oh, my God.'

Doing his best to avoid contact with the sticky web, the Doctor made a quick examination of the body. It was a man, and he'd been dead for some time. The Doctor ran his sonic screwdriver over the two massive puncture wounds in the man's shoulder. The flesh around the injury was green and diseased-looking, but that wasn't what had killed him. As far as the Doctor could tell, he'd died of a massive heart attack, and then something had dragged him here and cocooned him.

It was the 'something' that really worried the Doctor.

He tapped a finger lightly against one of the strands of web that held the corpse to the ceiling. Even with the lightest of touches it took considerable effort to pull his finger free.

The underpass was full of it. It had been the perfect place to trap prey.

He stepped back out into the daylight, mind racing. Somewhere in this peaceful-looking countryside there was a very, very big spider. Clara stood some distance away, chewing nervously on her fingernails. The Doctor couldn't blame her. The corpse wasn't a pretty sight. Visible through the veil of web, the man's face was contorted in fear and pain, lips drawn back in an awful grimace.

He walked back over to where she was waiting,

'Is he…?'

'Yes. Very.' The Doctor placed a hand on her shoulder and gently led her away from the underpass.

'Surely we aren't just going to leave him hanging there?'

'That web is incredibly strong, and I really don't fancy being caught up in it when whatever spun it returns.'

Clara looked around nervously. 'You think it's still around here somewhere?'

'It's possible,' admitted the Doctor. 'And on this occasion I'm not going to suggest that we just deal with it ourselves. We need to go into the village and get help.'

Clara nodded. 'All right.' She gave the Doctor a weak smile. 'I'm never going to complain about you taking me somewhere dull again.'

The two of them made their way down the footpath

into the village. Ringstone was picture-postcard pretty. Stone cottages, some with deep, thatched roofs, lined both sides of a wide, open village green dotted with trees and benches. In the centre was a tall limestone monument, a war memorial of some kind. A bright red telephone box stood outside a tiny village store, low stone walls bordered gardens brimming with flowers, and in the distance the stocky, stone tower of a Norman church poked up above the rooftops.

The Doctor looked around, quickly taking in his surroundings. 'Nothing here', he muttered to himself. 'There's nothing here…'

'That's a good thing, though. Right?' Clara was getting worried now. 'I mean it's got to be better for a giant spider to be here rather than in the middle of some heaving city centre, hasn't it?'

'That rather depends on what we're going to be able to find here to help us stop it,' said the Doctor ruefully. 'I can't exactly see the village store being equipped to handle a giant spider invasion, can you?'

The sound of a car door being unlocked made the Doctor look around. Not far away a woman had opened up the back of a Range Rover and was loading a large metal tray into the boot.

'Come on,' said the Doctor, 'We'd better break the bad news to the locals.'

Angela's head was still reeling with the implications of the creature that Gabby had brought into the surgery. She had quite reasonably assumed that she had been brought some bird or rodent that had made its way into the house or been hit by a car; a not uncommon occurrence in these parts. Nothing had prepared her for what had been inside the tea towel.

It was a common-or-garden crane fly – a daddy longlegs – but it was massive, nearly forty centimetres from wingtip to wingtip. Unfortunately, it had been quite badly mangled by Gabby in her panicked efforts to kill it. Even so, there was enough of it left for Angela to conduct a reasonably thorough examination.

Promising Gabby that she would let her know as soon as she had any more information, she had bundled the young woman and her children out of the surgery. Gabby was terrified that there might be more of the things in her house, but Angela had assured her that this had to be a fluke of some kind. There was no chance of there being more of them.

Only partially reassured, Gabby had headed off to wait for the hardware store to open, intending to buy as many cans of insect repellent as she could lay her hands on.

As soon as she had gone, Angela had discarded the tea cloth and laid out the remains of the giant insect on a stainless steel tray on the examination table. After a good half an hour dissecting and probing she had to admit that she was stumped. As far as she had been able to tell, everything about the insect was normal – everything except for its size.

Realising that there was a limit to how much of

an investigation she could make into the creature's origins on her own, she had decided to take it over to Dr Goodchild at the cottage hospital in Chippenham. With luck he would be able to help her perform some proper tests, possibly even using their ultrasound scanner. She had decided not to phone ahead and tell him she was coming. If she started to talk about giant insects he was liable to think that she was losing her marbles. It was better to just present him with the monstrous thing face to face.

She was loading the tray into the back of her car when she became aware of two figures – a man and a woman – walking towards her.

'Good morning.' The man had a Scottish twang to his voice.

Angela carefully pulled a cloth over the insect in the boot.

'Good morning.'

'Can you tell me if there's a police station in the village?'

'No. The nearest one is in Wyndham. But Charlie Bevan, the local constable, lives just across the green.' Angela frowned. 'Is everything all right? Has there been an accident?'

'Not exactly…' The man and the woman glanced at each other. 'You might have a slight insect problem.'

Angela felt the blood train from her face. 'Oh, no. Please don't tell me there are more…'

The man's bushy eyebrows rose quizzically. 'More?'

'You'd better have a look at this.' Angela lifted the

cloth from the steel tray. 'I doubt that you'll ever see a bigger insect.'

Clara perched on a stool in the corner of the vet's surgery watching as the Doctor and Angela bent over the examination table, peering at the huge insect lying under the bright lights.

It never ceased to amaze her just how quickly the Doctor managed to completely take control of a situation, whether it be on an alien planet or in an English country village.

As soon as Angela had revealed the insect, the Doctor had started firing off all kinds of scientific, biological questions, half of which Clara couldn't even begin to understand. Angela's relief at the realisation that she had someone to share her concerns with had been tangible. They had taken the mangled body back inside and the Doctor had listened as she had talked non-stop for nearly ten minutes about theories of mutations and chemical contamination.

Only when he had her complete trust did the Doctor finally – gently – break the news about the body that they had found in the underpass.

Angela went very quiet and pale. It took Clara a few moments to realise that in a community this small it was inevitable that the dead man would be someone that she knew, and probably knew well.

'I'm sorry.' The Doctor placed a hand on her shoulder. 'If it helps, I don't think it was the spider that killed him.

As far as I can make out he died of a heart attack.'

Angela just nodded. 'I think that I'd better get Constable Bevan.' She pulled on her jacket, shivering despite the warm spring day. 'Would you mind waiting here?'

The Doctor nodded. 'Of course.' As soon as Angela had gone, he pulled the sonic screwdriver from his jacket and started examining the dead insect once more.

Clara slipped off her stool and peered over the Doctor's shoulder. 'So, is she right?'

'Right?' The Doctor didn't look up. 'Right about what?'

'Mutations.'

He straightened, peering at the readings on his screwdriver. 'Yes and no.'

Clara folded her arms and glared at him. 'Well, that's a great help.'

The Doctor fixed her with a piercing stare. 'It *is* a mutation. But it's not a natural one. Someone has taken a great deal of time, and used a lot of very expensive equipment, to engineer this creature.'

'Engineer it?' Clara stared at him incredulously. 'You mean these things have been built?'

'Modified. The basic physiognomy would appear to be a naturally occurring species, but there are traces of recombinant DNA, growth hormones, synaptic enhancers.'

'But why? Why would anyone want to create these... things?'

The Doctor tapped the sonic screwdriver against his lips. 'I'm not sure...'

Their conversation was interrupted as Angela hurried back into the surgery, followed by a stocky, red-haired man in a police uniform.

'Doctor, Clara, this is Constable Bevan.'

Any doubts and questions that Charlie Bevan might have had died in his throat as he caught a glimpse of the daddy longlegs on the table.

'Oh, my good Lord. I thought... I thought this was some kind of...'

He pulled a large, white handkerchief from his pocket and wiped away the sweat beading on his forehead. 'I think you'd better show me where you found this body, don't you?'

Chapter
Three

A short time later, the Doctor and Clara were standing at the mouth to the underpass once more whilst Charlie Bevan took a closer look at the corpse. Angela had stayed at the surgery, saying that she wanted to continue her examination, but Clara could tell that it was just an excuse to avoid seeing first-hand what the spider had left. She couldn't say she blamed her.

'Be careful that you don't touch any of the web!' the Doctor called out. 'I don't want to be trying to cut you free if this thing returns.'

Handkerchief clamped over his mouth against the smell that was starting to build, Charlie made his way back over to them, his face grave.

'Any idea who it is?' asked Clara softly.

Charlie nodded. 'Alan Travers.'

'A local?'

'He owns… He *owned* a dairy farm a few miles away. Knowing Alan, he was probably on his way home after a night out at the Wheatsheaf.'

Constable Bevan reached for his radio. 'I should call this in, try to arrange for a search party of some kind to look for this creature.'

The Doctor caught the policeman's arm. 'Before you do that, I think that we should remove his body from the web.'

Charlie shook his head. 'The forensics team are going to want to examine it where it is.'

'He wasn't left hanging there just as a decoration,' said the Doctor coldly. 'This is a larder, and if our friendly neighbourhood spider gets hungry and comes back then there won't *be* anything left for the forensic team to examine.' He paused. 'Besides, I'd like to do an autopsy.'

Charlie looked at him curiously. 'Are you a doctor of some kind?'

'Of some kind, yes.'

'Well, I'm sorry. That's out of the question. We'll have to take the body to the hospital at Chippenham. Dr Goodchild can conduct the autopsy.'

The Doctor's expression darkened, and for a moment Clara thought that he was going to argue with him. Then, obviously thinking better of it, he released his grip on the constable's arm and regarded the body hanging in the tunnel once more. 'We're going to need help getting him down.'

Charlie indicated the pub just visible through the trees on the other side of the field. 'I'll go and get some help from the Wheatsheaf.'

'Good.' The Doctor nodded. 'Tell them to bring gloves,

and a ladder, and cutters of some kind. Secateurs, or garden shears.'

As Charlie hurried along the path towards the pub, the Doctor called out after him. 'And get something to wrap him up in!'

He turned to see Clara looking at him quizzically.

'Autopsy?'

The Doctor nodded. 'There wasn't enough venom in the puncture wound for me to make a proper analysis. I want to see if there are the same indicators of genetic tampering.'

'So you want to check that whoever engineered the daddy longlegs is the same person responsible for the spider?'

'Exactly.'

'Well, they'd better be, otherwise it's one hell of a coincidence!'

The Doctor smiled grimly. 'It can't also be a coincidence that the TARDIS brings us to this exact spot on the trail of a mysterious energy signature.'

'But what on earth can possibly connect giant insects, stone circles and ley lines?'

'I guess we're going to find out.'

The Doctor's eyes blazed and Clara felt a tingle of anticipation run down her spine. Despite the danger, despite the death, it was these moments that brought her alive, that made every second of her extraordinary life worth living. Her and her Doctor (and despite the changes to his outward appearance this *was* still *her*

Doctor), side by side, facing whatever the universe could throw at them.

A few moments later, the sound of a car engine made her look up, and she turned to see a battered Transit van pulling to a halt at the start of the footpath. Charlie Bevan and another man climbed out and walked up the path towards them.

'Doctor, Clara, this is Bert Mitchell,' said Charlie. 'He's the landlord of the Wheatsheaf.'

With old-school politeness, Bert shook both of their hands in turn, but even as he did so he couldn't tear his eyes from the cocooned shape that hung in the mouth of the underpass.

Clara felt a pang of remorse at her earlier excitement. The dead man was one of their friends, their neighbours. This wasn't thrilling for these poor people, it was terrifying. She tried to give him a reassuring smile. 'I'm sorry. This must be difficult to believe...'

'Difficult?' Bert shook his head. 'Impossible, more like.'

The Doctor, Charlie and Bert started to extricate the body of Alan Travers from the sticky web. Clara sat at the top of the railway embankment, keeping a lookout for any sign of the spider. Even with the heavy-duty shears that Bert had brought, the strands of web proved incredibly difficult to cut, and it took them several long minutes of hard work before they finally managed to pull the body free. Wrapping it in a sheet, the three men struggled down the footpath to the Transit and lifted the body carefully into the back.

Breathing heavily, Charlie wiped the sweat from his forehead. 'Wait here a moment, Bert. I'll just put a call in to the hospital, let Dr Goodchild know you're coming.'

As Charlie hurried across the green to the vet's office, Clara could see people starting to go about their business in the village, as yet unaware of the horror that was starting to unfold in their midst. Bert was obviously thinking the same thing.

'No one's going to believe it,' he said quietly. 'After all those jokes about them breeding monsters in the science park.'

The Doctor's ears suddenly pricked up. 'Science park? What science park?'

'The other side of the railway.' Bert nodded towards the distant embankment. 'Agricultural science research. New fertilisers, weather-resistant crops, bio-diesel, that sort of thing. Been a standing joke in the village that Jason Clearfield has been breeding monsters in there.' He shook his head. 'Never thought that it might turn out to be true…'

Clara exchanged a brief glance with the Doctor, but before they could question Bert any further, Charlie Bevan re-emerged from the vet's office.

'Is your CB set working, Bert?'

The landlord climbed into the cab of the Transit, started the ignition and switched on the set bolted to his dashboard. 'It seems to be. Why?'

'The phone lines are playing up. Mobiles too. Tune it

to the police frequency. Give me a call on that when you get over to the hospital. I've got a few things that I need to finish off here.'

Bert nodded, closing the door and pushing the van into gear. As they watched it make its way out of the village Clara turned to Charlie with a puzzled frown.

'CB? Do people still use that?'

Charlie nodded. 'Mobile coverage isn't too good out here, so CB is still popular with the farming community. Easy to use, easy to fix—'

The Doctor interrupted him. 'What was that about the phones?'

He shrugged. 'Interference of some kind. Couldn't get a mobile signal at all. Managed to use Angela's landline to get in touch with the hospital OK, but then the line went dead when I was on the phone to the Colonel.'

'Colonel?' The Doctor's voice went icy.

'Yes, Colonel Dickinson over at the army base at Warminster.'

The Doctor closed his eyes. 'No, no, no, no, no... Why did you have to go and do that?'

'I'm sorry?'

'Involve the army!'

'Because we have a giant spider stalking the fields and killing people? Who else did you think I was going to call? The local zoo?'

'Yes!' shouted the Doctor. 'That might have been a sensible idea! At least they might want to capture it rather than shoot it. What good is it to us dead?'

'What good is it?' Charlie's face flushed with anger. 'Now listen, I don't know who you are, but if you think that—'

'Stop it!' Angela Drabble stood in the entrance of the vet's surgery glaring at the two men. 'Stop it, both of you! You're squabbling like children!'

Such was the tone of the young woman's voice that both men went quiet immediately. Clara had to smother a smile with her hand. It was rare that someone had the authority to cut the Doctor dead like that. She was going to get on well with the village vet.

Angela marched over to them. 'That's better. We've quite enough problems without you two acting like a couple of farmyard cats squaring up for a fight. We've already lost one man, let's make sure that we don't lose any more.'

She pointed at the people making their way to and fro across the village green. 'We have to let people know what's going on. Get them to get their kids off the street, stay indoors, arm themselves if necessary.'

Sheepishly, the Doctor nodded in agreement. 'You're quite right.' He peered over at the church bell tower. 'Perhaps I can rig up some kind of shortwave radio transmitter. If I boost it through my sonic screwdriver, and if I can get the church bell to resonate at the right pitch, then we should be able to broadcast some kind of warning that everyone can hear.'

'Or…' said Charlie, 'we could just call a village meeting.'

*

'Corporal Jenkins! Have you managed to reconnect my call with Ringstone yet?'

'No, sir. The line is still dead.'

Colonel Paddy Dickinson sat back in his chair, a frown creasing his weather-worn features. What Charlie Bevan had just told him sounded utterly preposterous, and yet Dickinson had met the man on several occasions – most recently at the army v. police rugby game last month – and he had always seemed like a solid, dependable, professional policeman. He certainly didn't strike him as a man given to flights of fancy.

But giant insects?

After a few moments deliberation, he reached for the phone again. 'Jenkins? Get me Joint Helicopter Command at Andover.'

Ten minutes later, the Lynx was airborne, its two powerful Rolls Royce Gem 42 engines lifting it effortlessly off the tarmac and sending it hurtling above the English countryside at 180 knots.

The crew had been given only the vaguest of instructions – reconnoitre the area and report back anything unusual – but the fact that they had been scrambled in an AW159 Lynx Wildcat fitted with the .50-calibre M3M machine gun had given the mission a frisson of unexpected excitement.

Captain Jo Phillips, the pilot, couldn't understand it. She had been in Ringstone last month with her fiancé, a 'get to know you' day out with her future in-laws. The village was nothing but antique stores and teashops: nothing that could possibly warrant a military response of this kind.

She shot a glance at her co-pilot, Mike Vickers.

'What do you think?'

Vickers shrugged, unwrapping a stick of chewing gum and folding it into his mouth. 'Could be anything,' he said indistinctly. Vickers was half Bahamian, and invariably laid back about everything.

'Remember last month?' Leigh Brewster shouted from the cabin behind her. 'They scrambled us because some farmer thought that he'd seen a UFO? Stupid yokel.'

Phillips grinned. The UFO had turned out to be an advertising blimp that had broken loose from a big outdoor science fiction convention in Devizes. It had been painted up to look like the Millennium Falcon and had looked pretty good, so it was no wonder that it had caused a stir. But Brewster didn't have much time for the locals; he wanted to be back in the field. Phillips thought he was crackers. She'd seen enough of the deserts of Afghanistan to last her a lifetime.

Spotting the tower of Ringstone church poking up above the distant woodland, Phillips banked the helicopter, bringing it low over the fields.

'Right, let's see if we can work out what this is all about.'

Gabby Nichols stood at the back of the village hall listening with mounting panic as Constable Bevan,

Angela and a thin-faced, scary-looking man broke the news about the death of Alan Travers, and started to explain about the infestation of giant insects that seemed to be affecting the village.

If Gabby hadn't already witnessed one of the creatures first-hand, she might have thought that this was some kind of macabre practical joke. Several of the villagers around her were certainly of that mind.

'Come off it.' A voice that sounded like Simon George, the postmaster, rang out from the front of the hall. 'You must think we're soft in the head.'

There was a murmur of agreement from the room.

'It's a bit early for April Fool's Day,' called someone else.

'I realise that this must sound unbelievable,' Charlie Bevan was looking flustered. 'But there is a very real danger—'

'Of you looking like a total numpty,' finished Simon, eliciting laughs from the crowd. 'Someone's playing a bad joke on you, Charlie Bevan, and you've fallen right for it.'

'Then perhaps you would like to come to the hospital with us and examine the body for yourself.' The voice of the thin-faced man – the Doctor, he had called himself – cut through the room. 'No one is playing any jokes. These creatures are very real and very dangerous, and if you don't start listening to us then someone else in this room is probably going to end up dead.'

Now there was silence.

Charlie Bevan gave the Doctor a grateful nod. 'Thank you, Doctor. Now, here's what I propose we do... You've probably already realised that we have a problem with the phones. This seems to be affecting both landlines and mobiles...'

Gabby listened in a daze. That explained why she hadn't been able to get hold of Roy. She glanced at the display on her phone. It was the same as it had been for most of the morning: still searching for a signal.

There was a sudden tug on her trousers. 'When is that man going to stop talking, mummy?' Emily was looking up at her pleadingly. 'I want to go.'

That simple statement was like a light bulb going on in Gabby's head.

Her car was parked on the other side of the green. They could just leave.

Hoisting her sleeping son onto her shoulder, she grabbed hold of her daughter's hand and pushed her way out of the packed hall. Hurrying across the green, she scrabbled in her shoulder bag for the car keys. She'd misplaced them more times than she liked to remember since they'd moved house, so until she had got used to her new surroundings she'd taken to keeping them on her.

Grateful for her forward planning she unlocked the car, bundled Emily into the booster seat in the back and started to strap Wayne into his travel cot.

'Where are we going?' Emily had her puzzled expression on.

Gabby thought for a moment. She hadn't really given much thought to where they might go. 'Grandma's,' she said after a moment's thought. They could get to her mother's house in Wolverhampton in a couple of hours.

'Are we going home first?'

Gabby hesitated. Should she make a trip back home to pick up essentials? Wayne would need nappies and food. And Emily was only dressed in a light cotton dress.

She shook her head. They could always pick up what they needed en route. They'd stop at the supermarket in Devizes. She had her credit card and phone. As soon as she could get a signal, she could call Roy and tell him where they had gone.

'No, sweetie. We've got to go straight away.' She secured Emily in her chair, then slid into the driver's seat, fastening her own seatbelt and slipping the key in the ignition. To her relief, the car started first time.

As she pulled out onto the road, everything seemed so quiet and so normal that for a second she wondered if she was just being crazy. Then the recollection of Emily's screams at the daddy longlegs, and the horrible way that it had thrashed and writhed when she had swatted it from the window and tried to crush it, banished any doubts that she might have had.

Pushing the car into gear, she swung past the village hall and headed out of the village at speed. Usually she treated the narrow country lanes with caution but today she just wanted to get away from Ringstone as quickly as possible.

As they sped through the hedge-lined roads Emily gave a little 'whee!' of excitement. Gabby couldn't stop herself from smiling. Kids.

Her smile faded as she rounded a tight bend to find the road ahead blocked by a thick tangle of milky-white fibres. Gabby stamped hard on the brakes, but she was going too fast to stop in time. The little Fiat slammed hard into the web.

The impact knocked Gabby breathless. The inside of the car was a cacophony of screams. Recovering, she quickly checked the travel cot alongside her. Wayne was fine, just unhappy. She glanced in the rear-view mirror; Emily was still strapped in safely too. Satisfied that both of her children were unharmed Gabby, put the car into reverse. Tyres squealed noisily on the tarmac and the car lurched, but the web held them tight. Shifting into forward gear, she tried to push her way through instead, but the car just wouldn't budge.

Almost screaming with frustration, Gabby slammed the car into reverse again and pressed the accelerator fully down. Clouds of white smoke started to rise from the tyres as they span uselessly and, with a stuttering cough, the engine stalled.

Gabby slumped forward onto the steering wheel, trying to shut out the screaming from Emily and Wayne. What was she going to do?

A sudden noise made her start.

She looked up to see the strands of web just outside the windscreen starting to quiver, vibrate. She frowned.

What on earth could be causing it? Then, with a chill that reached deep into her gut, she realised that whatever had spun the web was coming to investigate what it had caught.

Fear galvanised Gabby into action. Unbuckling herself, she tried to open the driver's side door, but the web stopped it from opening fully. She started to wind down the window, then stopped. If the web was sticky enough to hold the car, then it would certainly be able to trap her if she touched it.

She twisted around in her seat. The car had slid into the web at an angle, and the rear passenger door was clear of any of the strands. Ignoring the wails of her daughter, she wriggled between the front seats, scrabbling at the rear door handle. The door opened and Gabby scrambled out onto the road.

Undoing Emily's seatbelt she hauled her from her seat, dumping her unceremoniously on the tarmac whilst she extracted Wayne from his cot. From somewhere behind her she could hear something large crashing through the fields nearby. She fought the urge to look around, concentrating on undoing the buckles and straps that held her son secure.

Three to go… Two to go… The last buckle came free and she wrenched Wayne out of the car. As she turned to grab Emily, she realised that her daughter had gone silent and was staring in terror at something over her shoulder.

Barely able to draw breath, Gabby slowly turned around. Two long, bristle-covered legs were reaching out over the top of the hedgerow. As she watched, something huge and dark started to haul itself onto the web. Gabby reached out for her daughter's hand, slowly backing away from the monstrous spider as its forelegs started to run over the metal roof of the car, trying to determine if this was food or not.

Gabby felt a sudden surge of hope. It hadn't seen them! It was more interested in the car. Her eyes flicked down to her daughter, and she put a finger to her lips.

To her relief, her daughter nodded and together they started to move away from the web. As Gabby tensed herself to start running there was a harsh buzzing from behind her and something landed hard on her back.

All thoughts of stealth abandoned, Gabby screamed and twisted, trying to shake whatever it was loose. Then there was a sudden, sharp pain between her shoulder blades, and her legs gave way beneath her.

As she slumped to the ground, she became aware of the dull drone of dozens of pairs of wings drowning out the screams of her daughter, and of a cloud of buzzing, hovering shapes closing in around them.

Only as she lost consciousness did Gabby remember the twelve cans of insecticide in the boot of the car.

Chapter

Four

As the village meeting started to break up, Angela came over to Charlie Bevan's side.

'Have you heard anything from Bert Mitchell yet?' she asked. 'Surely he should have got to the hospital by now?'

Charlie frowned. 'You're right. He should have called ages ago.' He unclipped the radio from his belt. 'Charlie to Bert, over?'

There was nothing but static from the other end.

Charlie tried again. 'Charlie to Bert, are you receiving me, over?'

'More interference?' asked Clara, concerned.

'No.' The Doctor plucked the radio from Charlie's hands and pressed it to his ear. 'It's working fine, there's just no one answering at the other end.' He handed it back to him. 'This hospital. Is it far?'

'Not very.'

'Then I suggest we go and see what they've been able to find out.'

'We can go in my car,' said Angela. 'I still want to get an

ultrasound scan of that crane fly.'

Leaving Simon George to wrap up matters in the village hall, the four of them made their way across the green to where Angela's big Range Rover was parked. As they approached the car, Charlie Bevan's radio suddenly crackled into life.

The policeman gave a sigh of relief. 'At last. Go ahead, Bert, over?'

'Please… Help…' The voice that issued from the speaker was weak, and obviously in pain, but it was the sound in the background that made Clara's skin crawl. Almost drowning out Bert's terrified pleas for help was the sound of rending metal and a high-pitched, hissing screech.

Angela clasped her hand over her mouth. 'Oh no…'

'Bert!' shouted Charlie Bevan. 'What is it? What's wrong?'

Bert's voice became a scream of pure terror, and then the radio went dead.

There was a moment of stunned silence, and then everyone dived into the car at once. Clara was barely able to close her door and fasten her seatbelt before Angela started the engine and set off at speed.

'Do you know where he is likely to be?' asked the Doctor as the Range Rover careered around the village green and raced off down one of the narrow country roads.

Angela nodded. 'This is the most direct route to the hospital. He'll have gone this way.'

Next to Clara in the rear seat, Charlie continued to shout into his radio, desperately trying to get back in contact with the pub landlord, but Clara could tell from the expression on his face that he already feared the worst.

As the car flew along the narrow road, the Doctor caught Clara's eye in the rear-view mirror. His expression said everything. This was about to get dangerous.

They hurtled around yet another tight bend and Clara was suddenly thrown forward in her seat as, with a screech of brakes, the Range Rover shuddered to an abrupt halt.

'Oh, my God.' Angela had gone very pale.

The Doctor was out of the car in a flash, motioning for everyone to stay where they were as he edged slowly forward down the road.

'To hell with that,' muttered Charlie Bevan. 'Bert might need help.'

Before Clara could try and stop him, he unclipped his seatbelt and hurried forward to join the Doctor, who turned and glared at him angrily, raising a finger to his lips.

Cautiously, Clara slid across the rear seat and stepped out into the roadway. The route ahead was totally blocked with a thick tangle of sticky, white web strung between the hedges and trees that lined the road. Bert's Transit van was on its side in the neighbouring field. He had obviously lost control as he tried to avoid the obstruction and had ploughed through the hedge. The windscreen was cracked, and steam was still rising from an obviously damaged radiator.

That in itself might have been bad enough, but the damage to the rear of the van was even worse. It looked as though something had torn the vehicle apart with a can opener.

Charlie started to scramble over the ditch towards the car, but the Doctor caught his arm. 'Just wait a moment.'

'But—'

'Wait!' snapped the Doctor, the tone of his voice making it quite plain that he was in no mood to be argued with.

Leaving Charlie Bevan half in and half out of the ditch, the Doctor made his way cautiously forward towards the web. Long, pencil-thick strands stretched off through the foliage to the higher branches of the trees. One eye on the treetops, the Doctor reached out and tapped a fingertip on one of the strands of web, tensing himself to run.

The web quivered slightly. Peeling his finger free the Doctor tapped it again. After the third tap he turned to the others.

'All right. It seems safe enough for the moment.'

The four of them clambered down into the field and Angela crossed to the Doctor's side. 'You thought that it might have been waiting? That it's using these webs to trap food?'

'Yes. But there's something erratic about the way this creature is behaving. The cocooning of the man in the tunnel was almost to be expected, just a spider trapping its prey in an enclosed space. This –' he jerked his thumb towards the web that blocked the road – 'this seems to have been put up deliberately as a barrier to stop people getting out.'

'Or anyone else getting in.'

The Doctor nodded grimly.

'Doctor!' Charlie had reached the Transit and was looking inside the buckled and twisted cab. 'There's no sign of Bert, or of Alan's body!'

The Doctor peered into the shattered rear, running his fingers over the jagged metal. It had been peeled back like the skin of an orange.

'There's blood on the windscreen.' Angela pointed at a smear of crimson on the shattered glass. 'There's no airbag in this old thing. If he's got a concussion then it's unlikely that he could have got far.'

'Um, he managed to get this far…' Clara was standing next to a shotgun. There were several spent cases lying on the grass next to it. 'Looks like he managed to get off a couple of shots at whatever it was that attacked him.'

'Then where is he?' asked Angela

'Dunno.' Clara reached down to pick up the discarded weapon, but as she did so she noticed something that made her hesitate. The barrel of the gun was bent, twisted, and partially melted into the grass. She withdrew her hand and took a step backwards.

'Perhaps not.'

Her nose wrinkled as the wind changed, and an acrid, acidic smell drifted across the field. Angela smelt it too, covering her nose with her hand.

'God, what *is* that?'

Trying to locate where the smell was coming from, Clara spotted a large, dark shape towards the middle of the field. It too looked soft, dissolved somehow. With a growing sense of dread, she started to make her way forward, trying to get a better look, but as she drew closer, the twisted, human outline of the shape became horribly discernible.

'Doctor!' Clara started to back away in horror, unable to tear her eyes from the warped shape that had once been a man. As she did she heard a cry of warning from the Doctor, and a scream of pure terror from Angela.

Clara looked up, and froze as a huge beetle burst from the trees ahead of her. It was vast, nearly as big as the Transit, its bristle-covered body wet and glistening. For a moment it stopped, antennae twitching, mouthparts audibly grinding together as it regarded its new prey.

Then, with a deafening, screaming cry, it lurched across the field towards them.

Chapter
Five

As the Lynx cleared the treetops, Captain Jo Phillips stared in disbelief at the scene unfolding in front of her.

'Holy Mother of God!' Leigh Brewster hauled open the side door to get a better look at the huge black and orange beetle lumbering across the field below them. 'Just look at the size of that thing!'

'Captain, looks like we've got civilians down there.' Her co-pilot pointed at four figures scrambling to escape the advancing monster. Phillips could see the remains of a wrecked Transit van, and an indistinct, but still recognisably human form in the grass below.

'Brewster, get that gun ready!' Phillips brought the Lynx swooping around, lining up the open side hatch with the thing below them. 'This is Army Air 179 to JHC headquarters. Hostile located. Possible civilian casualties. We are engaging.'

Any reply from her superiors was drowned out by the sound of Brewster opening fire with the M3M.

*

The Doctor and the others hurled themselves to the ground as the helicopter opened fire. The sound was incredible. Large calibre shells started to tear up the ground between them and the beetle, sending clods of earth showering into the air. There was a deafening screech of rage and pain as the bullets raked across the back of the creature, ricocheting off its armoured carapace and sending it reeling sideways under the impact.

Seizing the moment, the Doctor dragged Charlie to his feet, pushing him towards the sanctuary of the church visible through the trees on the far side of the field. 'Now! Whilst it's recovering! Run!'

Struggling against the downdraft from the helicopter's whirling rotors, Charlie staggered off as the Doctor looked around frantically for Clara and Angela. They were several metres away, still cowering from the onslaught of the roaring machine gun.

'Clara!' yelled the Doctor, barely able to hear himself over the noise. 'The church! Try and make it to the church!'

Clara nodded, grabbing Angela by the hand and scrambling to her feet. The two women started to run. Attracted by the movement, the beetle gave a hiss of anger and started to lumber towards them once more, mouthparts clacking hungrily. Another burst of machine-gun fire tore down from the hovering helicopter, but the beetle was now too far underneath for the gunner to bring the gun to bear properly, and the pilot wheeled away, trying to get into a better position.

With horror, the Doctor realised that the creature was now between him and Clara, and blocking their escape route.

'Clara! Freeze!' The two women skidded to a halt, still gripping tightly to each other. The Doctor started to shout, waving his arms. 'Hey! Over here!'

The beetle ignored him, still concentrating on its prey. Looking around frantically the Doctor picked up a rock and hurled it at the creature's back. There was a dull 'thunk' as it bounced harmlessly off the beetle's armoured shell. The Doctor watched helplessly as the creature stalked remorselessly towards Clara and Angela, its antennae twitching as it tried to locate them.

With a roar of engines, the helicopter swooped down once more, unleashing another barrage of shells. This time the bullets had an effect, shattering a section of the chitinous carapace and severing the tip of one of the monster's antennae.

Furious with the hovering thing that had hurt it and distracted it from its meal, the beetle turned towards the helicopter. As soon as its attention was directed away from them, Clara and Angela turned and ran in the opposite direction. The Doctor watched with relief as they scrambled through the hedge on the far side of the field. They might not have made it to the church, but they were safe for the moment.

The beetle was now hissing and screeching at the helicopter, rearing up on its hind legs as bullets continued to tear into it. Without warning, it turned suddenly, raising up its body and, with a sudden chill of realisation, the Doctor finally recognised what kind of beetle it was.

'Oh, no...'

With a hiss like a thousand fire extinguishers, a spray of milky liquid burst from the creature's abdomen, striking the helicopter broadside.

As soon as the spray hit them, Jo Phillips knew that they were in trouble. With a harsh crack, the acrylic windshield shattered into a spider's web of fracture lines, reducing her visibility to zero.

From behind her, she could hear Brewster scream as the liquid sprayed through the open hatchway, splashing across his face and body. She pulled back hard on the controls, sending the 'copter skywards, but the entire cockpit was starting to fill with choking, acrid smoke as the discharge started to eat into wires and cables. She couldn't begin to imagine what it might be doing to Brewster.

The stricken craft lurched as the beetle sent another jet of acid splattering across the fuselage. Warning lights started to blaze across the control panel in front of her. The joystick suddenly went slack in her hand, and with sudden, cold certainty Jo knew that all the control lines had gone. Seconds later the fuel lines were gone too and, with a cough of protest, the engines stuttered and died. The aircraft was now nothing more than several thousand kilos of metal and plastic with nothing to keep it in the air.

As the helicopter tumbled towards the ground, Jo caught a glimpse of the tower of Ringstone church, and wondered what it might have been like to get married there.

The Doctor ran as the helicopter plummeted from the sky, its metal skin hissing and steaming as the caustic mix of hydroquinone and hydrogen peroxide ate into the airframe.

It hit the ground on the far side of the field with an impact that knocked him off his feet. There was a brief moment of blissful silence, and then the fuel tank exploded, sending a ball of orange fire boiling into the clear blue sky. The Doctor covered his head with his arms as metal and burning plastic rained down around him. As the wave of scorching air swept over him, the Doctor scrambled back to his feet.

The monstrous beetle was pinned behind a wall of flames, screeching in anger at the prey that had escaped it. With a last helpless look at the burning wreckage of the helicopter, the Doctor turned and hurried across the field, then made his way through the trees and the neat, well-tended graveyard and into the church beyond.

He closed the ancient wooden door behind him and leant against it, using the cool calm of the church interior to try and gather his thoughts. Things were getting out of control. At least half a dozen people were now dead, and he was no closer to discovering why the village was infested with these monsters.

One thing was becoming clear – someone or something wanted this village cut off from the outside world.

He opened his eyes to see the frightened face of Charlie Bevan staring at him from behind a row of pews. Puzzled, the Doctor opened his mouth to ask what on earth he was doing, but Charlie shook his head frantically and pressed a finger to his lips. Then he pointed upwards.

The Doctor edged forward, peering up into the gloom of the church ceiling. The roof was a tangle of web, heavy with the bodies of cocooned sheep, and hanging amongst them, was the huge quivering bulk of an enormous spider.

The crash of the Lynx changed everything. Suddenly Ringstone was the most important place in the country. Almost every time Colonel Dickinson hung up his phone it started to ring again. He'd already taken calls from the Prime Minister's private secretary and the Secretary of State for Defence, both demanding to know what was going on. The colonel had to restrain himself from pointing out that if they stopped interrupting him with pointless phone calls and let him get on with his job, then he might have a better chance of finding out.

In the meantime his calls to UNIT were being met with polite but unhelpful responses. Apparently all UNIT troops were engaged in a crisis in the Canary Islands. Robots with spiked heads were emerging from the recently erupted El Hierro volcano.

Dickinson gave a snort of derision. Punk rock robots... Sometimes he didn't think the people at UNIT lived in the real world.

There was a knock on his office door, and he looked up impatiently as Corporal Jenkins entered. 'Yes, Corporal?'

'Land Rover waiting outside for you, sir.'

'Good.' The colonel nodded in satisfaction. He snatched his cap off the desk as his phone started to ring again. 'You'll have to hold the fort here, Jenkins. Tell these wretched politicians that I'll get back to them with what's going on as soon as I damn well know!'

Leaving his adjutant to deal with the on-going barrage of phone calls, Colonel Dickinson marched outside to his waiting vehicle. He clambered into the Land Rover and it set off with a lurch.

'Any idea what all this is about, sir?' asked the driver as they roared out through the camp gates.

'I wish I knew, Private' said Colonel Dickinson grimly. 'I wish I knew.'

Clara and Angela had been watching from the other side of the hedge, waiting for the helicopter to drive off the beetle, and for an opportunity to get back to the Doctor and Charlie. The crash had put paid to that. Clara had watched in horror as the stream of acid engulfed the aircraft, hissing and boiling as it burned through metal and plastic. Seconds later the rotors stopped turning and the crippled machine started to drop towards them.

Grabbing Angela by the arm, Clara dragged her into

the ditch alongside the road, hunkering down alongside her as the helicopter hit the ground and exploded with an impact that left Clara's ears ringing.

As burning aviation fuel set the hedge alight, she and Angela fled, hoping that they could get back into the village centre and make their way to the church from there.

They set off along the road and Clara took a last look back at where the column of acrid black smoke was billowing into the morning sky. 'You'd better not be under that lot, Doctor,' she murmured to herself.

The two women walked on in silence. The quiet of the English countryside that Clara had initially found soothing was now eerie and ominous. Every rustle of undergrowth or flutter of wings made her jump, fearful of another monstrous insect emerging from the hedgerows.

They passed yet another road cut off by swathes of white web. 'Something has been busy,' said Clara. She was beginning to realise that everyone in the village had been effectively corralled in.

Angela was looking in concern at where a car was trapped in the web, one of its rear doors hanging open. A handbag lay in the middle of the narrow road, its contents scattered across the tarmac. 'Do you think…?'

'Let's not, eh?' Clara caught her arm. 'Let's get to the church, and find the Doctor.'

'You put a lot of faith in him.' Angela looked her in the eye. 'Is it well placed?'

'Yes.' Clara held her gaze. 'It is. He will sort this.'

After a moment's pause, Angela nodded. 'Then let's get back to him.'

It didn't take them long to get back to the village centre, but even here the streets were disconcertingly deserted.

As they were about to make their way across the green a sudden noise made Clara start. Something small was moving from behind the war memorial, half hidden in the shadows cast by the two huge elm trees either side of it.

'Something's there,' she whispered, dragging Angela into the garden of one of the cottages that bordered the green. Crouching in the flowerbed they peered over the top of the low, stone wall as the small shape stepped out into the sunlight.

Angela gave a sigh of relief. 'It's all right. It's Emily Nichols.' She frowned. 'I can't see her mother, though...'

Angela started to rise from her hiding place but Clara caught her by her arm, pulling her back down. 'No, wait a moment, something's wrong.'

Angela shook herself free. 'What's wrong is that a little girl is out there on her own. I'm going to get her.'

Before she could move, the door to the Post Office on the other side of the green swung open and Simon George stepped nervously out into the street.

'Emily!' he hissed. 'Over here! Quickly!'

The little girl didn't move.

Obviously agitated, Simon hurried across the road towards her. He was constantly checking the sky above him. Clara followed his gaze. What was he looking for? He had almost reached Emily when the 3-year-old suddenly turned, raised her hand to point at him, and let out a horrifying, almost inhuman scream.

Almost immediately the air was filled with a deep throbbing hum, and half a dozen huge mosquitoes swept into the village green, their wings a blur of movement in the late-morning light.

Simon turned to flee, but he had no chance. The mosquitoes swarmed around him as he flailed out at them, but they always kept just of reach. Suddenly one of them swooped down, landing on his back, and Clara heard him scream in pain as the creature stabbed through his shirt with its needle-like proboscis.

The postmaster slumped to his knees as the mosquito lifted from his back, re-joining the rest of the swarm, rising high into the sky and vanishing over the rooftops. For what seemed an eternity, Simon knelt there, head bowed, and Clara was beginning to think he must be dead. Then, with almost puppet-like movements, his head jerked back upright, and he clambered unsteadily to his feet.

Clara and Angela ducked down, pressing themselves tight against the wall, as Simon and Emily started to move slowly towards them. All around the green, villagers were starting to appear, drawn by Emily's scream. They shuffled slowly forwards, arms hanging limply, their faces grey and sallow, their eyes unfocused and glazed. The zombie-like effect it had on the faces of the more elderly of the village inhabitants was bad enough; on the children like Emily it was simply terrifying.

Clara looked desperately at Angela. 'We've got to find somewhere to hide!'

Angela nodded towards a narrow passageway leading to the rear of the cottage. 'Through there.'

On hands and knees, the two of them scrabbled along the passageway, emerging into a small, neat patio garden. At the end of the garden was the steep grass slope of the railway embankment.

As they hurried across the lawn, another horrible wail came from the village green, followed by a recognisably human shout of terror.

Angela turned, her faced creased with uncertainty. Clara couldn't begin to imagine how she must be feeling, seeing her home invaded by monsters, her friends and neighbours attacked, violated.

'There's nothing we can do,' she said gently. 'If we go back, if we try to help, then we're lost too.'

'I know, I just feel so helpless.' Angela wiped the tears from her eyes with the back of her hand.

'I know. But we have to go. Now.'

Angela nodded, and the two women scrambled up the embankment, over the railway line and into the unknown of the fields beyond.

Chapter

Six

The Doctor lay on his back in the dark underneath one of the church pews, listening as the spider shifted around in the rafters above him. With his eyes closed and his hands clasping his sonic screwdriver to his chest, he looked for all the world like one of the stone knights that adorned the ancient sarcophagi ranged around the church interior.

From outside there had been disturbing sounds. High-pitched, almost inhuman screeches, the fluttering of wings, and all-too human screams of fear and pain. Whatever was happening to this village, it had entered the next phase.

Charlie Bevan lay under a pew a few feet away, dabbing at his face with his increasingly grubby-looking handkerchief. He had been desperate to get out of the church, but the Doctor was certain that if they tried to make a run for it they wouldn't get more than a few hundred metres, if that. Bizarre as it might seem with the spider hanging above them, as long as they remained undetected, this was probably the safest place in the village at present.

There was a sudden rustling noise from high above them, and the Doctor's eyes snapped open. The spider was moving, the harsh bristles that covered its legs and body scraping against the ancient timbers of the church roof as it squeezed its way back outside.

As soon as the Doctor was certain that the creature had gone, he and Charlie clambered out from underneath the pews.

'Thank God.' Charlie Bevan rubbed at his aching back. 'My stomach was starting to rumble and I was certain that monster was going to hear it.'

Motioning to the policeman to stay quiet, the Doctor crept over to the church door, carefully turning the huge iron handle and allowing the door to open a little.

The village was totally still – no voices, no traffic. Even the birds had fallen silent. The Doctor was about to slip outside when movement at the far side of the churchyard caught his eye. Several of the villagers were making their way across the green. The Doctor frowned. There was something wrong about the way they were moving. They were sluggish, their arms hanging heavy at their sides. As they shambled past the entrance to the churchyard the Doctor caught a glimpse of their faces. Every one of them was blank and staring, their skin grey, their eyes dull.

'What's going on out there?' whispered Charlie from inside the church.

The Doctor waved angrily at him to be quiet.

Suddenly there was a commotion from the far side of the green. There was the roar of an engine and a car sped from one of the lanes that crisscrossed the village.

As one, the zombie-like villagers turned and started to run towards the noise. The driver didn't have a chance. Every way that he turned, more of the villagers closed in on him. Eventually he tried to turn a little too fast, and there was the squeal of rubber on tarmac as he lost control of the car and went crashing into one of the dry-stone walls.

At once the assembled villages let out a ghastly howl of triumph, and there was the low thrumming of wings as six huge mosquitoes swept into the village square.

Struggling to untangle himself from the seatbelt and airbag, the driver had no chance to fend them off. As the Doctor watched, the villagers pulled open the door and hauled the helpless man from the vehicle, forcing him to his knees and exposing the nape of his neck.

At once one of the insects dived forward and there was a cry of pain as it delivered its sting. Almost immediately, the driver stopped thrashing and, as the group stepped away from him, he clambered stiffly to his feet.

At once the group started to disperse, the driver now part of the shambling horde making its way out of the village green.

The Doctor closed the church door. Things were starting to move too fast even for him. As he tried to make sense of this latest development, he mulled over everything that had happened over the last few hours; the signal detected by the TARDIS, the appearance of the giant insects, the sealing off of the village, the markings on the stones. Then there was the bombing raid that had occurred during the Second World War. There were so many disparate pieces of the puzzle, but as yet he could find nothing common to connect them.

Charlie Bevan was looking at him with concern. 'Something's wrong, isn't it? There's something really bad going on out there.'

Lost in his own thoughts, the Doctor just nodded.

Charlie wiped the perspiration from his face. 'I'll tell you this, Doctor. No one is ever going to make fun of old Robin Sanford and his war stories again.'

The Doctor turned to face him, an eyebrow raised. 'War stories?'

Charlie nodded. 'Robin was a private in the Home Guard back in the 1940s. He lives on a farm on the far side of the village. Been living there since he was a child. Used to come out on a Saturday night, have a pint or two too many, and start going on about how his platoon fought off giant bugs from outer space during the war. Became quite a laughing stock around the village. Tends to keep himself to himself these days.' Charlie tailed off. 'Never even considered that he might be telling the truth…'

'Thank you, Charlie Bevan!' The Doctor's eyes were blazing. That was the last bit of the puzzle he needed. Giant bugs from space. That just *couldn't* be a coincidence. 'This farm, how far is it?'

Charlie shrugged. 'A ten, fifteen-minute walk.'

The Doctor muttered an ancient Gallifreyan curse under his breath. Avoiding the insects was tricky enough as it was, but insects assisted by their human allies…

'You're not thinking of going out there…?'

'Do you want all this to stop?' The Doctor's voice was sharp. 'Because if you do then I need to find out exactly what is going on. Robin Sanford has information, and I need to talk to him as quickly as possible.'

'But we're never going to get through the village without being spotted!'

'I can show you a way.'

A nervous voice echoed around the deserted church. Charlie Bevan nearly jumped out of his skin. The Doctor spun around trying to locate where the voice had come from. The pale, frightened face of a young boy was peering out at them from underneath the heavy velvet drape that hung over the communion table.

'And how exactly are you going to manage that?' asked the Doctor, raising an eyebrow quizzically.

'There's a secret passage,' said the boy matter-of-factly.

'Of course there is.' The Doctor's face broke into a broad grin.

The Land Rover sped past mile after mile of stationary traffic, the frustrated drivers venting their anger by sounding their horns angrily and demanding to be told what was going on. Colonel Dickinson just ignored them. In the sky ahead he could see the column of black smoke that marked their destination.

At the head of the queue was a roadblock with two soldiers diverting the traffic along alternative routes. As the Land Rover approached, the soldiers sprang to attention, one directing them to park on a lay-by just outside the village perimeter. As the Land Rover crunched to a halt on the gravel, an officer hurried to meet them.

'Good morning, Colonel.' The officer saluted sharply.

'Captain Wilson.' Dickinson returned the salute. 'What's the situation here?'

'We've set up a forward command post, sir, and we have squads stationed at several points all around the village. Can't get in, though. See here.' The captain led them through the bustle of soldiers and equipment to where a sheath of web hung between two large elm trees, totally blocking the road in front of them.

The colonel reached out to touch it, but Captain Wilson caught his arm. 'I wouldn't do that, sir. Couple of the men tried to climb it when we arrived; we're still trying to cut the stuff off them. All roads into the village appear to have been sealed off the same way, the railway line too. Plus there's some kind of communication blackout. Landlines and mobile signals are both down. We've managed to boost RT signals, but it's very glitchy.'

'Any word from inside the village?'

'Not a peep, sir. We've had spotters checking from all around the perimeter. Definitely movement in there, but no communication in or out.'

The colonel nodded then glanced back at the queue of traffic. 'What are we telling the locals?'

'Simply that there was an accident during manoeuvres. For the moment that seems to be doing the job, but the longer the communication blackout goes on the more unlikely it is that our cover story is going to hold water.'

'And what about that?' The colonel gestured towards the column of smoke. 'Any chance of recovering survivors?'

'I'm afraid not, sir.' Captain Wilson shook his head. 'We tried to send a rescue team in, but…' He broke off. 'It's easier if you just see for yourself.'

He handed the colonel a set of binoculars and the two men climbed up onto the back of one of the Spartan armoured personnel carriers that sat grumbling in the roadway.

The colonel raised the binoculars and Captain Wilson pointed towards the church. 'In the shadows near the tree line.'

The colonel focused the binoculars, and then took a sharp intake of breath.

'Good God.'

The beetle lurking under the trees was huge. The size of a car. The colonel gave an involuntary laugh. 'A ruddy Volkswagen Beetle…'

'Yes. Bit of a monster isn't it, sir?'

'Have you tried to engage it at all, Captain?'

'Had one of the snipers take a couple of pot shots at it, but even with armour piercing rounds we're not making much of impression against it. Didn't want to open up with anything large calibre until we know a bit more about the whereabouts of the civilians.'

Colonel Dickinson studied the damage on the beetle's carapace. 'Looks like the Lynx might have had a bit of a go at it before it crashed, though. At least that means that these things are vulnerable. Have we identified the species?'

'Yes, sir. Dobby Palmer is a bit of a bug expert. Says it's a Bombardier Beetle.'

The colonel nodded. Corporal Nigel Palmer was one of their medics. Prominent ears and a distinctive nose meant that he had more than a passing resemblance to Dobby the house elf from the Harry Potter films, so the nickname had been inevitable.

'So, did Dobby tell us anything useful about this Bombardier Beetle?'

'Quite a lot, sir. Apparently this thing can squirt out boiling acid from its rear end. From what we can make out, it's probably what brought down the chopper. There is more, sir. Over here.'

The colonel climbed down from the Spartan and followed Captain Wilson to a tent that had been erected at the far end of the lay-by. Two soldiers lay on makeshift beds, their legs swathed in bloody bandages. Both men tried to rise as the officers entered the tent but Dickinson motioned to them to stay put.

'At ease.' His jaw tightened at the sight of the injuries. He had already lost the helicopter crew; he was in no mood to lose any more men. 'What happened here, Captain?'

'The web only seems to be blocking the main roads and footpaths into the village.' Wilson explained. 'The rest of the village perimeter is made up of open fields and hedgerow. Private Arnopp here volunteered to lead a party to try and recover the bodies from the helicopter. The squad didn't make it more than ten metres inside the perimeter.'

'More beetles?'

'No, sir, these.' Wilson indicated a table against one wall of the tent. Laid out in plastic containers were the remains of several large, shiny black objects. It took the colonel a few seconds to make sense of what he was looking at, then the various disparate parts suddenly became familiar.

'Ants?!'

'Yes, sir. They were burrowed in under the field. Took our men completely by surprise.' Captain Wilson picked up a tray with a section of abdomen in it. 'Vicious little beggars they are too. And tough. Private Arnopp emptied an entire clip into one of them before it went down. Even if you hack them up they keep on twitching. Had to use grenades in the end.'

The colonel took the tray from him, examining the body part. 'Do we have any indication yet of what might have caused these things to grow to such size?'

'Not a clue, sir. Lot of talk amongst the men about it being radiation, but that sounded a bit too much like the plot of a 1950s B-movie for my liking. Ran the Geiger counters over everything anyway, just in case, but readings are all normal. I've had one of the dead beasties biked over to the entomology department at Bristol University to see if they can come up with anything.'

The colonel nodded, placing the plastic tray back on the table. As he did so there were shouts from outside, and a low, thrumming noise, like an aircraft engine. The two officers glanced at each other in alarm.

'What now?'

They pushed out through the flap of the tent in time to see several large objects flitting at speed above the hedgerows. Squaddies scattered as one of the creatures swooped low over them, buzzing angrily.

As the creatures vanished over the trees, Colonel Dickinson turned to Wilson with a worried frown. 'Beetles as armoured divisions, spiders as sappers, ants as combat troops and now airborne support. These things seem to have a very good grasp of military tactics, don't you think, Captain?'

'Sir?'

'So far these things have only attacked if we venture inside their perimeter.' Colonel Dickinson stroked his chin thoughtfully. 'They're protecting something.'

He straightened.

'Captain, I want to know about everyone and everything inside that village. Who has gone in, who has come out, who lives there, who is on holiday there, who works there. Individuals, companies, everything.'

'Sir!'

As Captain Wilson hurried off, Colonel Dickinson watched the flying insects as they circled lazily above the distant church tower. Protecting something.

Or someone.

Chapter

Seven

Clara followed close behind Angela as she pushed her way through the brilliant yellow of one of the many rapeseed fields that quilted the countryside, trying to put as much distance between them and the village as possible.

As the sun rose higher in the morning sky, the air started to come alive with insects, and every buzz or flutter or rustle made Clara look over her shoulder in fear of what might have caught up with them.

Try as she might, she couldn't stop thinking about the poster of British insects that adorned the wall of the biology lab back at Coal Hill School, in particular the section on stinging insects. The spider and beetle and the mosquitoes were bad enough, but what if there were giant wasps or bees out here somewhere? She remembered the pain of being stung by a wasp when she was a little girl, and just thinking about the damage a giant sting could do made her feel nauseous.

As they made their way between the rows of gently waving plants, Clara suddenly caught sight of a series of low, prefabricated buildings sticking up above the hedges ahead of them, and she realised that Angela had been heading for the science park that everyone had been talking about.

They were approaching the edge of the field when Angela stopped, crouching down amongst the yellow flowers and peering through a dilapidated wooden gate at the grounds of the industrial estate ahead of her.

Clara hunkered down alongside her. 'I should have guessed that you were heading for somewhere specific.'

Angela shrugged. 'We're not going to last long if we stay in the village, but those things might not have reached here yet, and there are bound to be secure rooms where we can hide out, and a phone that we can use.'

'Unless "those things" came from here in the first place,' Clara reminded her.

Angela frowned. 'Mad scientists breeding giant insects in a secret lab in the wilds of the English countryside? Surely you don't believe that?'

'You'd be surprised just how much weird stuff I've started to believe recently.'

Angela stared at her curiously.

Clara shook her head. 'Ignore me. I'm just waffling. You're right, we should find somewhere secure. Can you see anyone?'

Angela took another look across the road. 'Looks dead to me.'

Clara took a deep breath. 'Well, come on, then.'

Clambering over the gate, the two of them raced across

the road and into the industrial estate. As they crossed the deserted car park, Clara suddenly realised just how exposed and vulnerable they were now that they had left the cover of the field. They hurried over to the nearest building, and she peered through the glass door into the vestibule beyond.

'Can you see anyone?' asked Angela, heaving uselessly on the locked door.

'Nope. Empty. We'll have to try another one.'

Keeping to the shadows along the wall, the two women made their way to the next building, but that too was locked and empty.

'This is stupid!' shouted Angela thumping her fist against the glass door in frustration. 'There are cars parked here, so where *is* everybody?'

Clara looked around the deserted science park with mounting panic. The longer the two of them stayed out in the open like this, the more chance there was of being spotted. They had to get inside, and quickly.

A sudden flicker of movement right on the edge of her vision made Clara start. There was something moving on the roof opposite. She whirled around, pressing her back hard against the aluminium skin of the building.

Angela's eyes widened in horror. 'What is it?' she croaked, unwilling to turn around and see for herself.

As Clara steeled herself to fend off whatever flying horror had tracked them down, she suddenly realised what it was that had caught her eye. 'It's all right!' she gasped in relief. 'It's just a security camera.'

Angela clasped a hand to her mouth, stifling an almost hysterical laugh.

The camera was one of several mounted on the corners of the buildings. As they watched, it swung down to point directly at them. As it did so, it struck Clara that this was no automated movement. It was being controlled. Someone was watching them.

She stepped out of the shadow of the building, looking directly up at the camera, and waving her arms frantically. 'Hey! Can you hear us? We're stuck out here. You need to let us in!'

For what seemed like an age, the camera stared impassively down at them, then a set of double doors on a building opposite swung open with a crash, and several figures emerged.

'Thank God,' breathed Angela, starting to turn towards them.

'No, wait.' Clara caught her arm. 'Something's not right.'

The figures heading towards them were dressed in white, one-piece overalls and lab coats. They moved with the same, limp-armed, shambling gait as the people back in the village.

'Oh, no.' Angela shook her head in despair. 'Not here too…'

Clara caught her by the hand. Angela was beginning to believe that it was hopeless, and if she started thinking like that then they were finished.

'Angela.' Clara's voice was stern. 'We have to go. Now!'

With the stumbling figures in pursuit, the two women started to run.

'Kevin?' Charlie Bevan stared at the boy in amazement. 'Kevin Alperton? What on earth are you doing down there?'

The boy scrambled out from under the communion table.

'Hiding from the insects, same as you.'

The Doctor squatted down so that he was face to face with him.

'But it's not just the insects that you're hiding from, is it?'

Kevin shook his head. 'It's everyone. Well…' He looked nervously at the Doctor and Charlie. 'Everyone except you two, I hope.'

'Well, there's no need to worry about us.' Charlie tried to give the boy a reassuring smile, and placed a hand on his shoulder. 'Eurgh!' He pulled his hand away in disgust. It was covered in a thick slime.

Kevin grimaced and gave the policeman an apologetic smile. 'Sorry about that. Insects can detect each other though their smell, so I was disguising myself.' He gave the Doctor a shy shrug. 'I saw it in a horror film called *Mimic*. Thought that it was worth a try.'

'Pheromone masking.' The Doctor gave him a nod of approval. 'Very enterprising. And where, might I ask, did you obtain the secretions to try this?'

Kevin opened his satchel, pulled out a battered

Tupperware lunchbox, and proffered it to the Doctor, peeling back the plastic lid. 'It's a bit bashed up.'

The Doctor reached into the box and gently extricated the mangled remains of one of the mosquitoes. Charlie Bevan gave a little squeak of alarm and retreated a few steps.

'It landed on my back, but I fell over and squashed it before it could sting me,' explained Kevin. 'I think that it's the mosquitoes that are turning everyone into zombies.'

Pulling his sonic screwdriver from his pocket, the Doctor laid the insect on the velvet drape of the communion table, and started to examine it. 'And I think you're right.' He gingerly lifted the needle like proboscis of the mosquito and sniffed at the clear liquid that beaded at its tip.

'Careful!' hissed Charlie. 'If that's some kind of venom…'

'Scopolamine.'

'I'm sorry?'

'It's Scopolamine. It's a drug that blocks the neurotransmitters that carry information to the part of the brain that stores short-term memory. It also makes people more open to suggestion. Josef Mengele used it in interrogations as a kind of truth serum. The CIA administered doses of Scopolamine during its controversial behavioural-engineering experiments in the 1960s.'

Charlie stared at the insect in disbelief. 'But that's—'

'It's all sorts of things,' snapped the Doctor angrily.

'It's irresponsible. Immoral. Dangerous. Criminal.' He turned to glare at Charlie. 'And it's deliberate. Someone is using these insects as tools.'

Further discussion was abruptly halted by the clatter of roof tiles from somewhere above them. The spider was returning to its lair.

The Doctor whipped around to face Kevin. 'This tunnel. Show us! Quickly!'

Unwilling to lose the means to disguise himself, Kevin scooped the mosquito back into the Tupperware box, snapped the lid on, and stuffed it into his satchel. 'This way.'

He led them to a wooden door in the far corner of the chancel. On the other side was a small vestry with yet another door leading through to the building at the back of the church. Kevin hurried through it. The rooms beyond were dark; the walls festooned with children's pictures and parish notices. Kevin scurried over to a heavy wooden door set under a flight of slightly rickety-looking stairs.

'It's down here.'

The door swung open with an almost theatrical creak, and Kevin fumbled in the dark for the light switch. A bare, energy-saving bulb faded into life, dimly illuminating a narrow stairway and damp stone walls. The Doctor and Charlie followed Kevin into the gloom.

The cellar was a mishmash of boxes, old furniture, camping equipment and carefully furled Cub Scout flags. Kevin pushed his way over to the far wall and pulled aside a battered sofa to reveal a small, dark opening.

'We discovered this last October,' explained Kevin. 'There was a Scouts Halloween party down here, and me and Baz Jones wanted to scare Akela. Must've got boarded up ages ago.'

The Doctor peered into the dark opening. 'How far does it go?'

'It comes out near the old water pump next to the Post Office.'

Charlie Bevan grimaced. 'That's not very far.'

'Well, it's better than nothing.' The Doctor snapped on his sonic screwdriver, lighting up the tunnel in emerald green light. 'You know where you're going, Kevin. You'd better lead the way.'

As Kevin scrambled into the tunnel, the Doctor turned back to look at Charlie. 'I think that it's time we got Mr Robin Sanford to tell us the whole story about his giant bugs from outer space.'

Clara and Angela huddled together in the shadow of a huge recycling bin, watching as the white-coated figures spread out across the industrial estate.

It had quickly become apparent that they had no chance of escaping if they stayed out in the open. Angela had been all for heading back to the village, but Clara had pointed out that they were no better off back there, and besides, she was now certain that whatever was going on had something to do with the science park. There was no other reason why someone should be watching them, but doing nothing to help them.

Now that her attention had been drawn to them, Clara had spotted dozens of cameras dotted around the site. That was when she had her idea. Most of the buildings seemed to be deserted. All except for one. Therefore it made sense that the key to finding out what was going on lay within that building. They had to get inside.

Angela had looked at her as if she was mad. 'You want to go *inside* the building that the zombie lab-coat people just came out of?'

Clara had just nodded. 'Got a better idea?'

Using parked cars as cover, they had started to make their way back towards the centre of the industrial estate, but there were too many of the white-coated figures for them to move freely. They had only just managed to make it to the recycling bins without being seen. They needed to send their pursuers off in the other direction.

Clara had been watching the security cameras, trying to determine some kind of pattern to their movements. She was sure that most of them were purely automatic, tracking to and fro on a pre-timed sequence. Presumably that pre-controlled movement could be overridden manually, as it had been when they were first detected, but she was banking on there being too many cameras scattered around the site for someone to control all of them that way.

From their hiding place she could see three of the cameras. There was a twelve-second window when all three of them were looking away from the bins where she and Angela were concealed. It must have been pure fluke that they had made it here without being spotted. Hoping that their good luck would continue to hold out, Clara took a deep breath, bundled up the cotton cardigan that Angela had been wearing, and waited for the next gap in the cycle.

'Any second now,' she whispered.

'Coast is still clear!' said Angela, scanning the car park.

All three cameras were moving into the perfect position. Clara tensed herself. Any second…

Now.

Launching herself forward from the cover of the recycling bins, Clara hared towards the hawthorn hedge that bordered the industrial estate. As she ran she counted under her breath. 'Twelve, eleven, ten…' If she wasn't on her way back by the time she reached five…

She skidded to a halt by the hedge, tossing the sweater so that it caught on the uppermost branches. Her heart caught in her mouth as it started to drop. It wasn't going to catch! To her relief, the spiky branches of the hawthorn finally snagged in the cotton, but her mental count was at four.

Clara turned and ran as fast as she could. She could see Angela's panic-stricken face staring at her from between the recycling bins. From the corner of her eye, she could see the cameras starting to sweep back around once more.

She wasn't going to make it.

Chapter

Eight

The Doctor squeezed through the narrow brick corridor, his mind still sifting through all the various pieces of the mystery that he had landed in. Scopolamine was the latest clue, and he was certain that the fact that it was a drug that had been used by the Nazis was significant.

The drug, the bombing raid, a Home Guard battalion stationed here in the war, an alleged battle with giant insects… Whatever had happened here during the 1940s was going to be key to understanding what was really going on. There was one more bit of the puzzle that he still didn't have, though.

The science park.

He stopped. 'Hold on a minute, Kevin.'

'What is it?' said Charlie's muffled voice from behind him. 'Is something wrong?'

'This science park. Tell me about it.'

Charlie stared at him incredulously. 'You want to talk about that *now*?'

'Can you think of anywhere better?'

'He's right,' said Kevin cheerfully. 'The bugs are never going to look for us down here, and no one in the village knows about it. No one except me and Baz Jones, that is... And his mate Derek Farmer. And perhaps the Roberts twins. But other than that...' He regarded the Doctor curiously. 'What was it that you wanted to know?'

'Bert Mitchell mentioned someone called Jason Clearfield. What can you tell me about him?'

'He wears a mask!' said Kevin, his eyes shining. 'Like in *The Phantom of the Opera!*' His face fell. 'The stage version, though, not the Hammer film. It would have been so much cooler if he wore a mask like the Hammer film. Or the Universal one—'

'Is this really relevant?' interrupted Charlie impatiently. 'Yes, the man wears a mask. Apparently he suffered horrific burns in an industrial accident. It doesn't mean he's some kind of a monster!'

'No, it doesn't,' the Doctor agreed. 'But it also doesn't mean that we should discount the possibility of him being behind this just because the idea of a masked scientist breeding giant insects seems improbable. We've already ascertained that these creatures have been tampered with genetically. That means access to laboratories, complex machinery and chemicals.'

'And don't you think that someone would have noticed that by now?' Charlie took a deep breath. 'Look, I was over there last week. Clearfield showed me around...'

'Why?'

'I'm sorry?'

'Why were you there?'

'An attempted break-in. Some of the locals had a bit too much to drink on Friday night and tried to force the door to one of the laboratories.' Charlie gave the Doctor a pointed stare. 'The idea that they're breeding monsters on the industrial estate is a *very* old joke around here.'

The Doctor was silent for a moment, then nodded, and the three of them continued their slow progress along the passageway.

Despite Charlie Bevan's reassurances, the Doctor had already decided where his next port of call would be after he had talked to Robin Sanford. He had an appointment with Jason Clearfield.

Calf muscles protesting at the effort, Clara threw herself forward, crashing painfully onto the tarmac as the camera finished it sweep and started its inexorable journey back the other way.

For several seconds she held her breath, waiting for any indication that she had been spotted, but the car park remained deathly quiet.

'You really like cutting things fine, don't you?' whispered Angela angrily.

Clara let her breath out in a rush and peered around the bin to look at where the bright red sweater fluttered in the midday breeze. 'Now we just have to see if it worked or not.'

Sure enough it didn't take long for someone to spot the flash of colour, and there was a whirr of servos as all three cameras turned to focus on the spot where the sweater was caught. Moments later there was the sound of heavy footsteps, and a dozen or so of the white-coated technicians appeared from around the corner of the far building.

One of them, a young man who Clara didn't think could be that much older than herself, reached up and tugged the sweater free.

'They have escaped into the fields.' There was no emotion to the voice. It was just a statement of fact. 'They must be trying to get back to the village.'

The man tilted his head to one side, almost like a dog listening to something, then nodded and started to push his way through the hawthorn hedge, seemingly oblivious to the sharp thorns that tore at his exposed face and hands. The others followed and soon they had formed a ragged line, spreading out through the fields as they searched for Clara and Angela.

Angela let out a deep sigh of relief, and was about to step out from their hiding place when Clara motioned to her to stay still.

'Wait…'

Moments later, several of the giant mosquitoes droned overhead, joining the humans in the fields in their search.

'All right, we've shaken them off,' said Angela quietly. 'So, how do we get inside? March up to the door and knock?'

'If the Doctor was here, I might just go with that,' said Clara wistfully. 'But I think I spotted another alternative.'

Checking that the cameras were still pointing at the gap that had been created in the hedge, Clara led Angela back through the industrial estate until they were looking once more at the building from which their pursuers had emerged.

'I noticed it earlier,' said Clara, pointing at a fire escape door set into the end wall of the building.

'OK…' Angela wasn't convinced. 'And you think that they're just going to leave it unlocked.'

Clara just smiled. 'Come on.'

They hurried over to the door. The metal frame on one side was scuffed and bent.

'Looks like someone has already tried to have a go at this…'

'That was some of the local farm hands,' explained Angela. 'It got a bit boisterous after karaoke night at the Wheatsheaf last week.' She pulled at the door half-heartedly. 'Well, what a surprise, it's locked. So, unless you've got a set of skeleton keys…'

'Nope.' Clara grinned at her. 'But I do have a hairpin!'

As Angela kept watch, Clara started work on the lock. Moments later it opened with a satisfying click.

Angela looked at Clara with surprise. 'There's more to you than meets the eye! Who taught you how to do that?'

'A young lady called Jenny Flint.'

'A professional thief?'

'Nope. Victorian chambermaid. Come on.'

Ignoring Angela's bemused expression Clara swung open the door. The interior of the building was dark and silent. Hoping that she wasn't making a serious mistake, Clara caught hold of Angela's hand and the two women stepped inside.

Kevin peered through the metal grille that marked the end of the tunnel, checking to see if there was anyone around. 'All clear,' he whispered, heaving on the ancient cast iron. The grille swung inwards and Kevin scrambled through, pushing the branches that concealed the tunnel entrance out of the way. The Doctor scrambled up after him followed by the Constable Bevan.

As the Doctor checked to see whether the coast was clear, Kevin regarded him curiously. He wasn't like anyone else he had ever met. He looked old – probably the same age as Kevin's grandfather – but there was something about the energy that blazed in his eyes that made him feel a lot younger.

No. Not younger.

Different.

Kevin shivered. He reached into his satchel, unclipping the top of the Tupperware box and scooping up some of the slime that coated the bottom. Being outside again was making him nervous.

Constable Bevan snatched the box from him. 'Don't use it all,' he said, puffing with the exertion of the climb through the tunnel. 'The Doctor and I are going to need some of that stuff too, you know.'

He scooped up a blob of the slime with his fingers and smeared it through his thinning hair.

'Blooming heck.' He grimaced. 'This stuff smells disgusting.' He held out the box to the Doctor. 'Your turn.'

The Doctor stared at him for a moment, and then lifted the silver tube that he had been using to light their way through the tunnel and twisted a tiny control set into its side. 'Or, I could just adjust the settings on this to generate a sonic umbrella that will create the same effect, but without the need for us to coat our scalps in the rotting juices of a dead insect?' He turned and gave Kevin the quickest of winks. 'Now, which way to Robin Sanford's house?'

Strangely reassured by the Doctor's wink, Kevin pointed down the road ahead of them. 'It's this way.'

Protected by the Doctor's sonic shield, the three of them made their way cautiously down the hedge-lined road. The further they got from the centre of the village, the narrower the road became, until it was no more than a single track, the tarmac surface cracked and full of potholes.

'Mr Sanford doesn't get a lot of visitors, I take it,' said the Doctor.

Charlie Bevan was looking nervously at the ever-more unruly hedges that were starting to close in around them.

'Like I said, he tends to keep himself to himself.'

'He came to our school once,' said Kevin, remembering a history class from the previous year. 'He was meant to be giving a talk about the Home Guard, but some of the other kids started to make fun of him. Asked him to tell them all about the giant insects and he got angry and had to be taken away by the headmaster.' He paused for a moment. 'I guess people might listen to him a bit more now. We should get him to come in again.'

As they reached the end of the road, the hedges started to give way to woodland and open fields once more. Robin Sanford's house was an old farm but, with the exception of the main house, all of the outbuildings were dilapidated and choked with ivy. Kevin remembered playing here with his friends when he was younger. To begin with Mr Sanford hadn't minded – in fact Kevin had vague memories of being shown things like old bullet casings and cap badges – but as the man got older he had become far less tolerant of people coming onto his property.

Motioning to Kevin and Constable Bevan to stay in the shadow of the encroaching trees, the Doctor made his way slowly across the farmyard towards the main door of the house.

He was about halfway across the yard when Kevin suddenly caught sight of movement in the doorway. The letterbox was swinging slowly open. As Kevin watched, two metal tubes emerged through the slot.

As the realisation of what the tubes were struck home, Kevin rushed forward, shouting out a warning.

'Doctor! Look out!'

His words were drowned out by the sound of both barrels of the shotgun firing in unison.

Chapter

Nine

The door closed behind them and Clara stood for several seconds, waiting for her eyes to become accustomed to the gloom of the interior of the building.

The area just inside the door was piled high with packing crates and discarded pallets. A forklift truck was parked against the wall, along with rack upon rack of heavy-duty electrical cable. Overhead, the ceiling was thick with chain hoists, and there was a metal walkway running around the interior of the building, access ladders positioned every couple of metres.

Clara edged forward though the boxes. The building seemed deserted, but ahead of her she could make out a circle of large, blocky shapes illuminated by a pale blue light. Keeping to the shadows near the wall, the two women started to make their way towards the light.

As they got closer they began to hear noises, a strange low electrical hum and other, more familiar sounds. Clicks and buzzes. Insect noises.

Against the far wall of the building stood dozens of

wire and glass cages. Some stood empty, their doors open, others still held huge monstrous shapes that clung to the wire mesh or buzzed and quivered in the middle of their cells.

Angela recoiled in horror. 'What are they?'

Clara had to admit that she didn't know. At first glance, she had thought that the creatures were enormous spiders, but as she forced herself to look closer she could see wings and scales, and far too many legs. It was as if someone had dismembered three of four kinds of insect and then stuck the parts back together in a different order. One of the creatures snapped at her lazily, and she jumped back.

Beyond the cages were benches heavy with complex scientific equipment, and a large glass window looked out into another room containing a sophisticated laboratory.

'Who is doing this?' whispered Angela angrily. 'And what on earth are they doing it *for*?'

'I don't know,' said Clara. 'But I'd be very surprised if it didn't have something to do with that.'

In the middle of the room stood thirteen big black boxes, each about the size of a single wardrobe, each with a large LED display set into the front. Arm-thick cables wound from the base of each to huge, grey bell-shaped machine, surrounded by consoles, CPUs and industrial-sized generators.

Letting go of Angela's hand, Clara started to make her way towards the humming monoliths. As she got closer she could see images flickering across the LED screens mounted on the boxes, patterns that seemed familiar somehow. It was only when she was standing in the middle of the circle that she made the connection. The patterns on the screens were the same as the patterns inscribed on the stones outside the village.

'It's the stone circle,' she breathed. 'Someone has built a technological version of the stone circle.'

'How very clever of you.'

The voice cut through the room like a gunshot. Clara shielded her eyes as lights all around the building snapped on, flooding the warehouse with a bright white glare. As the lights came on, the hybrid insects in the cages screamed their displeasure, filling the air with a cacophony of screeching and hissing. Angela ran to Clara's side as white-coated figures closed in on them.

'Cover those things up.'

As two of the figures hurried towards the cages, a tall man in an immaculate grey suit stepped into the centre of the circle. The first thing that Clara noticed about him was that he was holding what looked like a vintage Second World War service revolver. The second was that one half of his face was covered by a white plastic mask.

From the descriptions she had already heard there was only one person this could be.

This was the mysterious Jason Clearfield.

Only lightning-fast reflexes saved the Doctor's life. As the gun fired, he threw himself to one side, landing hard on his shoulder and rolling back onto his feet in one smooth, fluid movement. A muffled curse came from inside the house.

Sprinting forwards, the Doctor grasped the barrel of the shotgun and yanked hard. There was a loud thump and a grunt of pain from the other side of the door. Immediately the Doctor released the gun and pressed his sonic screwdriver to the lock, slamming his shoulder against the door as he did so.

It crashed inwards, and there was another cry of pain as his assailant was thrown to the floor. The Doctor pushed his way inside. An elderly man lay in the flagstoned passageway clutching at his shoulder. The Doctor snatched up the shotgun and glared at him with distaste.

'Well, it's good to see that you're following the traditional military model of shoot first, ask questions later.'

Charlie and Kevin pushed through the door behind him, the constable hurrying forward to help the man to his feet.

'What on earth did you think you were doing, Robin? You could have killed us!'

'Thought that your were some of them, didn't I?' The old man grimaced with pain. 'Thought you'd come to turn me into another zombie.'

'Oh, well, that's all right then,' snorted the Doctor contemptuously. 'It's perfectly fine to try and kill your friends and neighbours despite the fact that they are being used to do things against their will.'

Robin shot him an angry look. 'No friends of mine out there.'

The two men glared at each other for a moment, then Robin gave a deep sigh.

'You'd better come in.' He turned to Kevin. 'You, boy, close the door. And make sure you lock it properly. Don't want any of those creepy crawlies getting in.'

Robin led them down the hallway to a large, homely kitchen. An open box of shotgun cartridges lay on the ancient oak table that dominated the room. The Doctor handed the shotgun to Charlie.

'Here. Much as I dislike these things, it seems foolish not to keep it. Just in case.'

Charlie took it with a nod, snapping it open and removing the spent cartridges. Robin sat down heavily on one of the kitchen chairs, rubbing at his shoulder, obviously still in discomfort from the fall he had taken.

The Doctor crossed to his side. 'You'd better let me have a look at that.'

'Why? Some kind of doctor, are you?'

'Yes, as a matter of fact.' The Doctor started probing the muscles around Robin's shoulder, ignoring the grunts of pain that he produced. 'Nothing seems to be broken.'

'No thanks to you,' grumbled Robin. 'Still, I suppose that's something. It's going to stiffen up something rotten, though.'

'Not really.' The Doctor adjusted the settings on his sonic screwdriver and ran the tip over Robin's shoulder, filling the kitchen with a low warbling noise. 'You'll have a nasty bruise for a while but, other than that, you're as good as new.'

Robin moved his arm experimentally, and then looked up at the Doctor in amazement. 'Well, I'll be blowed...'

The Doctor pulled up another chair and sat down opposite him, elbows on the table, chin cradled in his hands and eyes blazing with energy.

'And now, Mr Sanford, perhaps you'd like to tell me about your experiences fighting giant insects during the war.'

'Excuse me, sir?'

Corporal Palmer stood in the entranceway of the mobile command centre.

'Yes, Corporal?' Captain Wilson looked up gratefully from the laptop, feeling the tendons in his neck pop as he did so. He hated desk work.

'Gunshots heard inside the perimeter, sir.'

Colonel Dickinson immediately looked up from his own computer screen. 'Gunshots? Where?'

'South side of the village, sir. Shotgun, most likely.'

'Then we'd better have a look. Get my Land Rover ready, would you, Palmer.'

'Sir.'

As the corporal hurried away, Dickinson leaned back in his chair, pursing his lips thoughtfully. 'What do you think, Captain? Resistance inside the village?'

Wilson shrugged. 'There are enough farmers with

shotguns so it's hardly surprising that someone would let fly at one of these things eventually.' He paused. 'If I'm honest, I'm surprised we haven't heard more.'

'Which suggests that there has been some kind of suppression of the locals.'

'Possibly. Assuming that the rest them aren't dead.'

The colonel was quiet for a moment, then he got up and shut the door to the command centre.

'Captain, what I am about to tell you is confidential. It concerns a *Wunderwaffe*.'

'Sorry, sir.' Wilson shook his head. 'Languages were never a strong point.'

'A Wonderweapon. A top-secret Nazi technological device known as *Die Glocke*.'

Captain Wilson looked at him blankly. '*Die Glocke?*'

'The Bell.'

'The Bell?' Charlie Bevan looked puzzled. 'What the devil is that?'

Robin Sanford got unsteadily to his feet, crossed the kitchen and pulled a battered and ancient-looking mug from a rack, dropping a teabag into it and setting it down next to an equally ancient-looking kettle.

'During the Second World War, the British army intercepted a coded radio signal. At the time they were trying to break the German U-boat cyphers, and everyone assumed at first that it was just some new ultra-complex encryption. The problem was that the signal didn't come from the North Atlantic, it originated in deep space.'

'You've got to be joking!' huffed Charlie dismissively. 'German propaganda, surely?'

'A lot of people thought the same at the time, but then they started to get reports from agents inside Europe indicating that the Germans had detected this signal too, and they were close to translating it.'

Robin watched the kettle boil, lost in his memories for the moment. The Doctor sat and waited, quite happy to let him tell the story in his own time, but Charlie was impatient.

'Well? What did it say?'

'It took the best minds months to get even a rough translation. Turing, Welchman, Knox... They all had a crack at it. They even had Judson working on it for a while.'

The Doctor stiffened at the mention of that name. 'Judson?'

'Yes, before he got whisked off to work on the ULTIMA project.' The kettle turned itself off with a click and Robin poured the boiling water into his mug. 'It was a set of instructions for building a machine, a huge metal bell, about twelve feet tall. Nobody had the slightest idea what it was for, but the Germans had already started construction, so we had no choice other than to start building one too.'

'You must have been very young at the time,' said the Doctor.

Robin nodded, sipping at his tea. 'I was 18. Denied active service because of a hereditary heart defect. Was made a private in the Home Guard here in Ringstone, though.'

'I thought that the Home Guard only defended beaches and things,' piped up Kevin.

'Quite right, young man. But they also guarded important military installations.'

'Like Ringstone,' said the Doctor quietly.

'Yes, Doctor. This is where the British Army constructed and tested their version of the Bell.'

Colonel Dickinson sat back down at his computer. 'Once I started asking questions about Ringstone it started all sorts of alarm bells ringing higher up the chain.' He gave a wry laugh. 'No, pun intended.'

He brought up a series of files showing plans, blueprints and grainy, black-and-white photographs.

'*Die Glocke* was the most secret of the Nazi weapons programmes, conducted in the dying months of the war. Code-named "Project Chronos", it was under the command of an SS General named Hans Kammler. The Nazis were getting desperate by this point, and were convinced that this was some kind of super-weapon, or new kind of aircraft, or antigravity device.'

He enlarged a series of aerial pictures of a factory complex set in a barren, mountainous area of northern Europe.

'They built their device in what is now Poland, at the Wenceslas mine in the Sudeten Mountains. A local dam was used to generate hydro-electric power for the experiments and inmates from a nearby concentration camp were used as workforce for construction of the test site.'

Wilson leaned forward and pointed at an indistinct circular shape on the aerial image. 'What's this? It looks for all the world like…' He broke off, suddenly feeling foolish.

'Yes?' The colonel looked at him expectantly.

'Well, it looks like Stonehenge.'

'Quite right, Captain Wilson.' Dickinson tapped a key and another picture flashed onto the screen, a modern-day image of a huge, circular, concrete structure, standing in the centre of an overgrown tarmac expanse. 'The Germans called this "the Henge" or "the Fly Trap". It was where *Die Glocke* was tested and is all that's left of the Chronos project.'

Captain Wilson sat back in his chair, his face a mask of confusion. 'I'm not sure I understand, sir. Nazi super-weapons and stone circles?'

Colonel Dickinson closed the laptop. 'The Nazis had fundamentally misunderstood the nature of the machine. Hitler was delusional, convinced that it was some ultimate weapon bestowed upon them by aliens to help him win the war. A lot of people were killed because of that belief. Several scientists died on the first operation of *Die Glocke*. Even with refinements to the machine and protective clothing, five of the seven scientists who conducted later experiments died from their exposure to it.' His expression hardened. 'And that doesn't even start to cover the number that were exposed to it deliberately, or the workers who were murdered by the SS at the end of the war to keep it secret.'

'I'm assuming that the British experiments were more successful?'

The colonel nodded. 'Apparently, it wasn't just a question of building the machine, it was a question of finding the right kind of energy to power it. In the end it was Aleister Crowley who solved the problem for the Allies.'

'The occultist?' Wilson struggled to keep the incredulity from his voice.

'He was working in counter-intelligence at the time, and suggested that our experiments were having more success that the German's because they were conducted in proximity to ley lines.'

'I'm sorry, sir,' Wilson rubbed at his jaw. 'I'm having a hard time believing all this.'

'Quite agree, Captain. Took me quite a while to get to grips with it myself. The point is Crowley was right. The experimental results did significantly improve when the machine was placed along ley lines. The Germans must have come to that conclusion themselves towards the end, but because of the location they had chosen for their test site they had no means of testing that hypothesis. There is some evidence of a possible incursion made by an SS commando squad to a Neolithic circle in Scotland with a much smaller Bell prototype sometime in 1944, but I'm not cleared to view those files.'

'So, our machine was located at Stonehenge?'

The colonel shook his head. 'Too obvious. The Allies knew that the Nazis were keeping tabs on the experiments, so they needed to find somewhere a little more off the beaten track. Ringstone was chosen as the British test site. Code name "Project Big Ben".'

'Using the local stone circle? The King's Guards?'

'Exactly.' The colonel leaned forward. 'The machine wasn't a weapon, Captain. It was a teleport device. And it worked.'

Chapter

Ten

Clara watched the man carefully as he stepped into the circle, trying not to show how taken aback she was by the mask that he wore. Made of a semi-translucent white plastic material, it fitted tightly to his scalp, completely covering the left hand side of his face, and continuing down beneath the collar of his shirt. The skin visible at the edges of the mask was red and puckered and, just visible through the translucent material, she could make out dark, twisted patterns.

The man's left hand was clad in a black leather glove. It, like everything else about him, reeked of expense.

'Nice suit,' said Clara, trying to recover some composure.

'Thank you.' The mask half obscured the smile that the man gave her, but Clara could tell that it was without warmth.

She held out her hand. 'I'm Clara.'

Clearfield ignored her proffered hand, keeping the pistol levelled. 'I know who you are, Miss Oswald. I had a background check run on you as you as soon as you showed up on our security cameras.'

Clara lowered her hand. 'Of course you did.'

'You're a very enterprising young woman. Avoiding the insects in the village, breaking in here with such ease, sending my colleagues off on a wild goose chase.'

'Colleagues?' Angela gave a snort of derision. 'Surely you mean slaves?'

'Please.' Clearfield winced theatrically. 'Slaves is such a disagreeable word.'

'So is Nazi,' said Clara looking pointedly at the swastika emblazoned on the side of the bell-shaped machine. 'Wartime souvenir or family heirloom?'

'If you think that I have any sympathies for the Nazis or for what they stood for, then you are quite mistaken,' said Clearfield, his voice hardening.

'So the trappings of the Third Reich are just a fashion statement? A decorative decision?' She wandered over to the machine, rubbing her chin with her hand. 'I'm not so sure, red and black are so last year…'

'Don't try and pretend that you are stupid, Miss Oswald.' Clearfield snapped. 'I might not approve of the Nazis and their sickening regime but, like the Americans in the post-war years, I am more than happy to put my scruples to one side on order to take advantage of their scientific expertise.'

'All right. So you're a fan of German engineering.'

'A very specific example of German engineering. Only two of these devices have ever been made. One was destroyed, a very long time ago. The other…' Clearfield placed a gloved hand on the machine, caressing the surface gently. 'The other has taken years of research, and a lot of money to track down.'

'So this was built during the war.' Angela watched as Clara walked around it slowly. 'What does it do?'

'It's a gateway.'

'A gateway?'

'To another world.'

Angela gave a nervous, laugh. 'You have got to be joking…'

Clara shot her a quick look. 'Angela…'

'Interesting…' Clearfield regarded Clara carefully. 'That concept doesn't completely surprise you.'

'We are wasting time, Clearfield!'

The voice that boomed around the cavernous space was low and sibilant, a wet, burbling hiss that made Clara's skin crawl.

'Yes, of course.' Clearfield was immediately contrite. 'I'm sorry.'

Clara stared at him in horror. 'What was that?'

Clearfield took a deep breath. 'That, Miss Oswald, was the voice of the Wyrresters.'

'Aliens?' Charlie Bevan stared at Robin in disbelief. 'Aliens from another planet?'

'Coool!' Kevin's eyes were shining with excitement. 'I wish you'd told *this* story when you came to talk to us at school.'

'Quiet, both of you!' The Doctor leaned across the table eagerly. 'What happened when you turned the machine on? What came through?'

'Something… horrible.' Hands trembling at the memory, Robin took a sip of tea, spilling some of it down his shirt.

'Describe it, man!'

'Huge… Savage… We never stood a chance!'

'I have to know!'

Robin's eyes suddenly widened as the Doctor leaned close. 'Oh, my God… It's you…'

The mug slipped from Robin's fingers, shattering on the flagstones. Clutching at his chest he lurched towards one of the kitchen cabinets, reaching for a bottle of tablets.

Charlie scrambled from his chair and hurried to help him. 'Leave him alone! You're going to give him a heart attack!' He shook several of the white tablets into Robin's hand, and filled a glass of water from the tap.

Robin took it gratefully, slumping back into his seat and gulping down the tablets, his eyes not leaving the Doctor.

The Doctor had launched himself from his chair and was pacing around the kitchen. 'I have to know the species! Planet of origin!' He stopped, eyes narrowing as a thought struck him. 'There's no other choice,' he muttered to himself. He spun to face Robin once more. 'Can you remember the date? The exact date this happened?'

Robin stared at him, disbelief on his pale face. 'The twenty-first of March 1944. It's difficult to forget the day all your friends died.'

'The vernal equinox…' The Doctor snatched a quick look at the calendar handing on the wall. 'And it can't be a coincidence that today is also the equinox. That's what all this is heading towards…' He turned to Charlie Bevan. 'We need to get to my TARDIS, right now.'

The policeman just looked at him, uncomprehending.

'A blue box,' explained the Doctor. 'On the other side of the village…'

Charlie wasn't listening, instead he was staring past the Doctor's shoulder, his eyes widening. 'I don't think that's going to possible at the moment.'

The Doctor whirled around to see a huge, grey bulk creeping slowly across the kitchen window. With a crash, the kitchen window splintered inwards and a huge leg probed the room.

The shots and raised voices had drawn attention to them.

The spider had found them.

Captain Wilson sat in silence as the Land Rover sped through the narrow country lanes. He had had a lot to take in over the last fifteen minutes or so. Nazi super-weapons, secret wartime experiments. An alien invasion of Ringstone, for God's sake! But it was the news that followed that had really scared him.

It had puzzled him as to why they hadn't just made

a concerted effort to breach the perimeter. Giant beetle or not, he was certain that with the Spartan, and some of that experimental insecticide that he'd had delivered from the barracks at Warminster, they'd have little problem securing a defendable position within the village with relative ease.

The colonel had made it quite clear why not.

Dickinson had received direct orders from the MoD that if a Bell device was found to be operational in Ringstone, then he was to evacuate the surrounding area, pull his men back and call in an airstrike. A nuclear strike was out of the question, but permission had been given to deploy the latest generation of thermobaric tactical weapons.

An Apache attack helicopter was already being fuelled at Andover and fitted with two of the new variant Hellfire AGM-114N missiles. A cold sweat prickled over Captain Wilson's skin. He'd seen first-hand the effects that just one of these weapons could cause. The effects of detonating two of them over a village like Ringstone…

He consoled himself with the fact that for anyone still trapped inside the perimeter it would at least be quick.

The Land Rover pulled to a stop, and Wilson followed the colonel to a lay-by that gave an elevated view of the southern part of Ringstone. A squad of half a dozen men was deployed along the low wooden fence running along the edge of the roadway, their attention focused on something happening in the field below. Wilson was pleased to see that Private Arnopp was amongst them.

The colonel noticed him too. 'Glad to see you back on your feet, Private. How's the leg?'

Arnopp saluted stiffly. 'Bearing up, sir. Dobby – I mean Corporal Palmer – patched me up fine.'

The colonel nodded in approval.

Wilson stepped forward and peered over the fence at the farmhouse that nestled in the fields below them. 'What have we got here, Private?'

'Shots heard about ten minutes ago, sir. Civilians spotted at the farmhouse down there. Then the bug showed up.' He handed Wilson a pair of binoculars. 'On the roof.'

Steadying his elbows on the wooden fence, Wilson adjusted the focus. The huge spider was crouched on the roof at the far end of the farmhouse, long bristle-covered legs probing at the windows and doorways as it sought to gain entry. 'And I thought Iraqi camel spiders were bad,' he muttered.

He straightened, handing the binoculars to the colonel. As he did so, another shotgun blast echoed across the fields. Immediately each of the soldiers raised their weapons in anticipation. There was a blood-curdling shriek of pain and anger from the spider and it jerked backwards, sending roof tiles tumbling into the cobbled yard. Then, enraged by the things inside the building that had hurt it, it started to batter at the building with its forelegs.

'I think that we should give a bit of help to whoever is inside there, don't you, Captain?' said Colonel Dickinson.

'Yes, sir.' Glad to finally have a chance to engage the enemy properly, Wilson turned to Private Arnopp. 'Private. Seems only fair that you should get a bit of payback. Spider on the roof down there. Fire at will.'

'Thank you, sir.' Arnopp grinned at him. Stepping forward he brought his SA80 assault rifle up to his shoulder and squinted through the sights. Seconds later semi-automatic gunfire shattered the late morning air as Arnopp unleashed a hail of bullets at the spider.

The Doctor, Charlie, Robin and Kevin dived for cover as the spider thrashed outside the window, sending shards of glass and timber flying.

Charlie struggled to bring the shotgun to bear again, but before he could fire there was the distant chatter of rifle fire, and the farmhouse shuddered as the ancient walls took the impact of high velocity shells. The spider fell away from the window shrieking in pain.

The Doctor sprang to his feet. 'This is it! This is the only chance we're going to get.'

Between them, Charlie and the Doctor dragged Robin to his feet, hauling him out of the kitchen and towards the front door. 'No, wait... My pills. I need my pills.'

Kevin darted back into the kitchen and snatched up the old man's bottle of pills from the wreckage strewn across the floor. As Robin leaned on the banisters for support, Kevin ran back and handed the bottle to him.

'Thank you, lad.' Robin looked across at the Doctor. 'Leave the boy with me. You two lead that thing away.'

The Doctor said nothing, his mind weighing up all the alternatives.

'We both know that I'm just going to slow you down,' Robin insisted. 'Once it's gone, we can barricade the windows, make this place secure. You need to go.'

The Doctor nodded. 'It's not going to stay distracted for long, and on foot we're a sitting target. If we're going to lead it away from here, we need transport of some kind!'

Robin leaned over to the coat stand next to the door and fumbled in the pocket of a mud-spattered Barbour jacket. 'Can you ride a motorbike?' he asked, holding up a set of keys.

The Doctor grasped them gratefully 'Yes!' His face immediately fell. 'No! I think so. Maybe.' He glared angrily at Robin, as if this confusion was somehow his fault. 'I don't know! I haven't had a proper chance to find out what this body can do yet.'

Robin just looked at him as if he was mad.

'I can,' said Charlie Bevan quietly. 'Basic police training.'

The Doctor stared levelly at him. 'Are you sure?'

Charlie shrugged. 'You need to get to this TARDIS thing of yours. A motorbike is going to be the quickest way of getting there.'

The Doctor tossed the keys to him. 'Good man.' He hauled open the front door. 'Let's go.'

'Captain, we have civilians in the open!'

'Cease fire, Private!' Wilson snatched up the binoculars

and quickly located the two figures racing from the front door. The spider was still at the rear of the house, momentarily confused by Arnopp's bullets.

As Wilson watched, the figures crossed the yard to one of the dilapidated outbuildings, one of them fumbling with the chain and padlock that secured the faded wooden doors. The chain fell away and the doors were hauled aside, and the squeal of ancient hinges was audible from even this distance. Immediately the spider tensed, obviously alerted by the noise. Cautious now, it started to crawl around the farmhouse, making its way slowly to the yard at the front.

'Come on, come on…' Wilson murmured as he watched the two men vanish into the gloom of the outbuilding. Whatever they were up to, they needed to do it quickly otherwise they were going to be trapped.

For what seemed like an age there was no movement other than the slow, relentless crawl of the spider. Then, suddenly, there was a loud, throaty roar from inside the building and Wilson had to stop himself giving a cry of delight as a vintage Norton Big 4 motorcycle and sidecar, still in its original military olive green, burst out of the open doors.

Aware that its prey was out in the open, the spider launched itself forward, moving at frightening speed.

'Private!' yelled Wilson. 'Give those men covering fire!'

Arnopp's assault rifle roared into life once again, and bullets raked across the farmyard, stopping the spider in its tracks.

That hesitation was all that the two men on the motorcycle needed. Tyres squealing on the cobblestones, the powerful side valve engine sent the Norton speeding across the yard and out onto the road beyond.

Bellowing with rage and pain, the spider vanished into the trees, trying to catch up with its quickly disappearing prey.

Wilson lowered his binoculars and turned to one of the waiting soldiers with a grin of triumph. 'Get on the RT, Private. See if we can find out where those two are heading!'

Chapter
Eleven

Clara watched with concern as Angela was led away by two of Clearfield's white-coated 'colleagues'.

The young vet gave a despairing look over her shoulder as she was pushed through a doorway in the corner of the warehouse, leaving Clara and Jason Clearfield alone.

Clearfield followed Clara's gaze. 'Please don't worry about her, Clara. I may call you Clara? I've no intention of hurting your friend. I just want to ensure that I have your co-operation.'

'I suppose that you didn't intend to hurt those poor people in the village either?'

'They are drugged. Nothing more. I would have preferred to have had the entire village evacuated before this evening's solstice, but…' He shrugged. 'My resources to achieve that are somewhat limited. Trust me, I intend to hurt nobody.'

'Tell that to Alan Travers,' said Clara angrily. 'Or Bert Mitchell. Or the crew of that helicopter. Those monsters that you've created are killing people!'

Clearfield turning away, his face flushing. 'That's not my fault. There have been problems, the creatures are not always easy to control!'

'And that makes it all right?' asked Clara incredulously.

'You don't understand the difficulties that I have faced—'

'*Enough!*'

The vile gurgling voice boomed through the warehouse one more.

'*Why do you waste time on this endless bickering?*'

'It is important that she understands!'

'*Do you presume to argue with me?*'

'No. No, I'm sorry, but please... If I can just explain to her what we are trying to do...' Clearfield turned to Clara, indicating one of the chairs next to a control console with the pistol. 'Sit down, please.'

Clara looked pointedly at the pistol.

With an apologetic smile Clearfield slipped it back into a holster beneath his jacket.

'Thank you.' Clara perched on the edge of the seat. 'I'm all ears.'

'An experiment took place here during the Second World War. A British experiment that was intended to put us in touch with creatures from another planet...'

The Doctor clung to the sidecar for dear life as Constable Charlie Bevan drove the vintage motorcycle at breakneck speed through the narrow country lanes. Behind them he could hear the spider as it crashed through the undergrowth, but its speed was no match for the Norton and soon they had left it far behind.

With the noise that the old bike was making, however, they were likely to attract the attention of everything else in the village, human or otherwise. The Doctor fumbled in his pocket for his sonic screwdriver, activating the sonic shield. That should keep them safe from the mosquitoes at any rate.

Charlie leaned over and shouted above the roar of the engine. 'Where are we headed?'

'The big meadow just beyond the stone circle,' the Doctor yelled back. 'When you get there, just head for the police box!'

'The what?'

'Just drive!'

Charlie twisted the throttle and the Norton hurtled forwards. Before long they were back at the village green and Charlie brought the bike coasting to a halt in the lane alongside the Post Office.

'What have you stopped for?' asked the Doctor in irritation.

'Look,' whispered Charlie, pointing to the far side of the green.

A huge crowd of people – men, women, children – was standing motionless in the centre of the village. Several of the huge mosquitoes were perched on the top of the war memorial, basking in the sunlight, or clinging to the stone sides, their wings occasionally filling the air with a low drone.

'It looks like the entire village…' breathed Charlie in amazement.

The Doctor tapped his teeth with his sonic screwdriver. 'Is there another way to get to the meadow?'

'We could take the ring road, but there's no telling whether it's going to be passable.'

'Then we're just going to have to go through them.'

Charlie looked at him in horror. 'You're not suggesting that I run them down?'

'Of course not!' snapped the Doctor. 'Just concentrate on keeping this thing on three wheels, and let me worry about clearing the way.'

He twisted the barrel of his sonic screwdriver, making careful adjustments to the settings, altering the sonic shield that he had been using to protect them from the mosquitoes to operate on a much wider scale. He needed to be careful. These people were unwitting participants in the events that were unfolding. He wanted something that was painful, but not damaging. He also had to focus the beam so that he and Charlie weren't affected.

Satisfied that the settings he had would give the desired effect, he turned to Charlie Bevan. 'Right. Let's see what this can do.'

Directing the screwdriver towards the waiting crowd, he pressed the activation stud. The effects were instantaneous. The crowd of villagers reeled, clutching at their ears.

'Go!' yelled the Doctor.

Charlie threw the Norton into gear, sending it roaring

across the village green. A few at the edge of the crowd made half-hearted attempts to reach for them as they swept past, but Charlie proved to be an experienced bike rider, and managed to manoeuvre the big Norton so that they were always just out of reach.

As they cleared the edge of the crowd, Charlie gave an unexpected whoop of delight. 'We made it!' His exultation was short lived as he took a quick glance in his wing mirrors. They might have eluded the crowd, but the insects were another matter.

The mosquitoes launched themselves from the war memorial and set off in pursuit. Gunning the engine, Charlie sent the motorbike and sidecar racing towards the footpath out of the village. As they passed through the narrow gap in the wall, there was the grinding shriek of metal against stone and the mudguard tore off the sidecar.

The Doctor gave him a reproachful look. 'Somehow I doubt that Robin Sanford is going to let you borrow his bike again.'

Twisting around in the sidecar, he pointed his sonic screwdriver towards the swarm of giant insects following them. Buzzing angrily, they swooped away, unable to stay in close proximity to the sonic wave that the Doctor was generating.

The bike swept past the circle of standing stones, bouncing along the footbath before finally emerging into the meadow where the TARDIS had landed.

'What on earth?' spluttered Charlie as he caught sight

of the incongruous blue box. 'That's never been there before!'

'Just keep going!' yelled the Doctor, dropping back down into his seat, adjusting the controls on his sonic screwdriver yet again and pointing it at the TARDIS. 'Drive straight at the doors!'

The Norton shot across the field, sending up clouds of white seeds as the tyres tore up the dandelions that carpeted the grass. The warble of the sonic screwdriver was joined by the high-pitched scream of Charlie Bevan as the bike hurtled towards the waiting police box.

At the very last moment, the doors slammed open and the Norton screeched to a halt in the control room beyond, dandelion seeds slowly settling around it as Charlie cut the engine.

The Doctor was out of the sidecar in a flash, closing the doors and hurrying over to the control console. 'Clara does that with a lot more style and a great deal less noise.'

Charlie dismounted from the bike, staring around the interior of the TARDIS in awe. 'It's—'

'Bigger on the inside, smaller on the outside, defies all the laws of physics, totally impossible, blah, blah, blah…'

'It's a time machine, isn't it?'

The Doctor looked up from the controls in surprise.

Charlie gave him an exhausted smile. 'That's why you were so keen for Robin to tell you the exact date, wasn't it? You want to go back and see what happened?'

'Yes,' said the Doctor, regarding Charlie Bevan with a new respect. 'That's exactly what we are going to do.'

He pulled down hard on the dematerialisation switch and the huge rotors above the console started to turn. 'Welcome aboard!

Chapter

Twelve

Private Robin Sanford of the 14th Wiltshire (Ringstone) Battalion Home Guard took one final look over his shoulder to check that no one was watching him, then leaned forward and struck a match on the rough dry-stone wall.

As the match head flared into sputtering life, and he raised it to the tip of his hastily constructed roll-up, a gruff, gravelly voice boomed from the darkness behind him.

'Those things are going to be the death of you, Private Sanford. That's assuming that I don't kill you first, of course.'

Cursing his luck, Sanford let the cigarette drop into the mud, crushing it under the heel of his boot and snapping to attention as Sergeant Desmond Hughes stepped into the stone circle.

'Just what do you think that you are doing, Private?' The sergeant's voice growled like distant thunder.

'Thought I heard something, sir!'

'Oh, really?' The sergeant thrust his face close to Sanford's, until their noses were practically touching. 'And just what was it that you thought you heard, you horrible little man?'

'A wheezing, groaning noise, sir!'

'A wheezing, groaning noise?'

'Yes, sir! And I think I saw a flashing light. Thought that I should check.' He gave the sergeant a cheeky grin. 'Might be that spaceship that Mr Churchill is always telling us to look out for.'

The sergeant took a long look around the moonlit fields. 'Well, I don't see any spaceships or flashing lights, Private. And the only wheezing and groaning that I want to hear is from you helping the rest of the men unload our top-secret government experiment from the truck! Do I make myself clear?'

'Yes, sir!'

'Well then, hurry along! At the double!'

As Sanford turned away, Sergeant Hughes stopped him.

'Private Sanford…'

'Sir?'

'Stay alert. There's something a bit queer about all this. Doesn't smell right to me. Just… Just keep your eyes open.'

Puzzled, Sanford just nodded, and then hurried away to where the rest of his battalion were struggling to unstrap the huge metal bell from the back of a Scammell truck.

Sergeant Hughes took one last look around the field. Apart from the restless shuffling of the cows it was as quiet as the grave. He gave a scornful sniff. 'Wheezing, groaning noise, my hat.'

Turning the collar of his coat up against the strengthening wind, the sergeant went to re-join his men.

Crouched amongst the cows in the field, the Doctor watched as the sergeant vanished into the inky blackness. Hunched in the grass alongside him, Charlie Bevan was still trying to come to grips with what had just happened to him.

'It really worked,' he said, more to himself than anyone else. 'We really have gone back in time, haven't we?'

'It's 21 March 1944,' said the Doctor calmly. 'I told you that I needed to find out exactly what happened here on that day.'

'And I thought you meant finding a decent library or something.' Charlie's voice was starting to become slightly hysterical. The Doctor turned to face him, placing a hand firmly on his shoulder.

'Constable. I realise that you have been through a lot over the last couple of hours, but I need you to stay calm and stay focused.'

Charlie pulled his now filthy handkerchief from his pocket, wiped his face and took a deep breath. 'So, we're going to try and stop them doing whatever it is they're about to do, I suppose?'

The Doctor's face grew stern. 'The events of tonight

are already part of history. Immutable. We cannot change one moment of what is about to happen, do you understand me? We are observers, nothing more.'

Charlie nodded. 'Well, I suppose it can't be any more dangerous than where we were before, eh?' he said with a nervous smile.

The Doctor just stared at him.

Charlie's smile faded. 'Oh…'

The Doctor pointed to the stone circle. 'Back in your time, one of those stones has been replaced with a concrete bollard. There is a plaque on it. Can you recall what is written on that plaque?'

Charlie shrugged, puzzled by the question. 'The history of the stones. When they were built and why, the reason why there are only a few of them left…' He tailed off with the sudden realisation of what he was saying. 'The circle was destroyed during a German bombing raid during the Second World War!'

The Doctor nodded, and then raised a bony finger to point at the overcast sky. From above the clouds, Charlie could hear the distant drone of a plane.

Sergeant Hughes heard the plane too. He made his way back towards the village, glancing nervously at where half a dozen men were unloading the Bell onto a trolley. As he did so, he could make out the shape of one of the 90cm carbon arc searchlight units, sitting in the centre of the village green.

'Private Sanford!' he bellowed.

Sanford hurried over, with the perpetual expression of a man who had just being caught doing something he shouldn't have. 'Sergeant?'

'Why isn't that light over at the decoy site?'

Being spotted from the air had always been a risk. They were maintaining a complete blackout in the village, but there was only so far that could go. When they fired up the Bell, the purple glow that it created was likely to be seen for miles. Intelligence reports indicated that the Germans had some idea of what they were up to, and roughly where, so it had been decided that the best way to ensure the safety of the test site was to set up a decoy site several miles away. Hughes had sent a team out into the middle of nowhere with instructions to construct something that would look right from the air, and then illuminate it with searchlights. With any luck the Luftwaffe would waste all their bombs destroying several square miles of Salisbury Plain.

'Private Gould thought they had enough, sir,' explained Sanford. 'Spoke to them half an hour ago. Said that they have enough to light the place up like it's Christmas. They even managed to find an old church bell to finish things off. It should fool Jerry properly!'

Hughes grunted. 'Well, you can tell Private Gould that if I wanted him to start using his initiative I'd have asked for it! I want that light shifted as soon as he's able. If this cloud cover gets any thinner and that spotter plane comes over again then I want Jerry to be able to see that decoy site from the Moon.'

'Sir!' Sanford hurried off to the RT room they had set up in the village hall. As he did so, a big, black Austin staff car pulled up into the village green and the thin figure of a young man emerged from the rear door.

Hughes cursed under his breath. 'Great. The egghead. Just what we need.'

Picking his way cautiously along the mud track towards the stone circle, the man made his way over to where the sergeant was waiting.

'Sergeant Hughes! Why isn't this machine in position yet? It should have been on the ground ten minutes ago.'

'My men are working on it now, Professor.'

'The timings *are* crucial, Sergeant!' The professor glared at him from behind wire-rimmed spectacles. 'If we don't turn on this machine at the exact moment of the vernal equinox…'

'I am well aware of that, sir,' said the sergeant firmly. 'But ground conditions have meant that it has taken slightly longer than anticipated to get the control vehicle into position. I have drafted in extra men to make up the time lost. And there was a fifteen-minute contingency.'

The professor made a disgruntled 'harrumphing' noise, and then took a deep breath. 'I'm sorry to snap, sergeant. I realise that you are doing your best under difficult conditions.'

'Would you like to check the controls, sir?' Hughes gestured to a large grey vehicle parked a few hundred metres from the circle.

The scientist nodded and the two men started to

make their way across the wet grass. 'I gather that the equipment was heavier than you had expected.'

'Considerably. We didn't have anything big enough to shift it, other than one of the local tractors, and I didn't really want to involve civilians unless it was absolutely necessary. In the end we borrowed a converted Matador from the RAF boys at Lyneham.'

The two men stepped to one side as a soldier hurried past them, unfurling thick cable from a drum.

'Where are the civilians, by the way?' asked the professor. 'I saw no one on the drive in.'

'Evacuated to Chippenham. We've let Military Intelligence deal with the details and cover story. And good luck to them, the locals are a feisty bunch.'

'They'll thank us for it in the morning, Sergeant. By tomorrow, the eyes of the entire world will be on the village of Ringstone.'

The professor reached out for the door handle of the control vehicle.

As he did so, Sergeant Hughes rushed forward to stop him. 'No, sir! Don't!'

It was too late. The door swung open and brilliant yellow light lit up the field around them.

As the light from the open doorway illuminated the scene in front of them, Charlie Bevan gave a gasp of disbelief.

'That's not possible!'

The Doctor twisted around to look at him. 'What?

What's wrong?'

'That man…'

'The scientist?'

'Doctor, I know who that is!'

'Well done. So you know some of your local history.'

'No, you don't understand. I've met him. He was standing in front of me less than three days ago. That's the man who owns the industrial estate outside Ringstone. That's Jason Clearfield.'

Chapter

Thirteen

From the village there were distant calls of alarm. 'Hey! Put that bloody light out!'

Pushing past Clearfield, Sergeant Hughes quickly reached inside the door of the control truck and located the light switch, plunging them into darkness once more.

'I'm sorry, sir. You couldn't have known. We're operating blackout protocols. Two knocks so that the team inside know to turn the lights out before anyone opens the door.'

Clearfield looked sheepish. 'Of course. A sensible precaution.'

There was the sound of boots kicking up stones as Private Sanford hurried across the field towards them. 'Don't you bloomin' boffins know the meaning of the word blackout?' He skidded to a halt as he spotted Hughes. 'Oh! Sorry, Sarge…'

'It's all right, Private. Everything is under control here. How are we doing with that Bell?'

'The boys are ready to put it into position and connect

it up, sir.'

'Good.' Hughes nodded in approval. 'Perhaps you'd better supervise the final positioning, Professor?'

'Yes, Sergeant. Very good idea. Lead on, Private.'

As Sanford led the professor to where the Bell was being set up, Sergeant Hughes looked up at the ominous sky once more, checking for any indication that the German spotter plane had been alerted to their position.

'Scientists…' he muttered. 'They shouldn't be allowed out.'

The Doctor watched as Clearfield made his way across the field towards the hulking shape of the British Bell.

Charlie Bevan was adamant in his assertion that this was the same man that he had seen alive in 2014. Even without the mask, he was instantly recognisable.

The Doctor rubbed at his chin. One possible explanation was that this experiment had something to do with time travel. There was only one way to find out.

'I've got to get a look inside that van,' he whispered.

'Are you crazy? You can't just walk down there and start poking about!'

'Why not?'

'Because it's the war! If you get caught then they're liable to shoot you on the spot as a spy!'

'Good point.' The Doctor took a long look at what Charlie was wearing. 'If memory serves me correctly the British policeman's uniform hasn't changed significantly since 1944. This isn't quite right though.' He reached out and fiddled with Charlie's hair, pulling it into an approximation of a side parting. 'There! That and the fact that it's almost pitch black should fool most people.'

'You just want us to head down there? In plain sight?'

'I'm not suggesting that we go out of our way to draw attention to ourselves, no. But if we *are* spotted we just act as if we own the place. That always works.'

'OK. Even if we assume that I can pass for a wartime policeman, what about you? What are you meant to be?'

The Doctor tousled his own hair and waggled his eyebrows fiercely. 'Would you believe mad scientist?'

Charlie stared at him. 'Do you know what? I'd have no problem believing that whatsoever.'

'Excellent!'

Before Charlie had any chance to object, the Doctor scrambled to his feet, and started to make his way along the edge of the field towards the spot where the Matador was parked. As the first spots of rain started to fall, Charlie struggled to his feet and hurried after him.

'No, no, no! It needs to stand *exactly* on the ley line than runs between the church, the circle and the spire at Wyndham.' Clearfield removed his glasses and pinched the bridge of his nose in exasperation. 'Didn't you get the briefing document that I sent?'

'All right, Prof, keep your hair on. We got your document, but it wasn't exactly an exciting read, now was it?' Sanford winked at the rest of the men. 'Hardly "Health and Efficiency".'

Clearfield pulled a handkerchief from his jacket pocket and wiped the raindrops from the lenses of his glasses, trying to keep his temper. 'Well, Private, if you *had* bothered to read it then you would realise that the positioning and distance of the Bell from the stone circle is vital to its correct functioning, so if you would please just—'

'Yeah, it's odd that,' said Sanford, deliberately interrupting him. 'The lads and I thought that it would make much more sense to put the machine in the *middle* of the circle. You know? Round peg in a round hole? I mean, stands to reason, doesn't it?'

'Does it really?' Clearfield slipped the glasses back into his nose. 'Do you know what would happen if we put the machine in the middle of that circle and turned it on, Private Sanford?'

Sanford shrugged and opened his mouth to reply but Clearfield cut him off.

'All the plant life within a hundred yards would lose its chlorophyll, turning white in seconds. Any animal life nearby would die as all the soft tissue in its body crystallised. Imagine that, Private: your lungs, your heart, your brain, all turned to crystal before you could even draw breath. Then your corpse would start to dissolve, break down until nothing remained was a thick, black slime, then that too would dissipate until there was nothing left of you whatsoever. That is the mistake that the Nazis have made at their test site in Poland; that is what has happened to the test subjects that they have exposed to their Bell, and that is what will happen here if this machine isn't put exactly where I tell you to put it.'

There was utter silence amongst the assembled soldiers. Then one of them crossed himself with a trembling hand.

'Fortunately you have someone on your side who has understood the nature of this machine far more clearly than the Germans, so would you please accept that I know what I'm doing, and get on with your work?'

Sanford held Clearfield's gaze for a moment, then looked down at his boots. 'Yes, sir.'

As Clearfield watched the soldiers hurry away to get the Bell positioned, he let out a deep breath. He had never been good at confrontation. It reminded him too much of time spent at boarding school facing up to boys far bigger, and far more stupid than he was.

'Nicely done, Professor.' A voice at his shoulder made him start. It was Sergeant Hughes, an amused smile on his face. 'You should have enlisted. You'd have made a good officer.' He paused. 'How much of what you just told them was actually true?'

'All of it, Sergeant. Position the Bell too close to the circle and it becomes a massive mutation generator. If this goes wrong, then everyone here is going to die.'

'And if it goes right?'

Clearfield leaned back and looked at the sky. 'Then we will never look at the universe in the same way again.'

The Doctor cautiously made his way across the field

towards the control van, Charlie following behind. The rain was starting to fall more steadily now, turning the ground under their feet into a quagmire.

As they reached the parked vehicle, something on the passenger seat of the cab caught the Doctor's eye. Opening the door he reached inside and pulled out a clipboard and a technician's lab-coat. As he shrugged into the brown coat, he plucked a pencil out of Charlie's breast pocket and stuck it behind his ear.

'Always helps to have the right props. Wait here, I won't be a jiffy.'

With that he ducked around the back of the van, knocking twice on the door. There was the sound of muffled movement from the other side, then it opened and the Doctor slipped inside.

The interior of the control vehicle was crammed with a bewildering array of complex electronic equipment. The Doctor was impressed. For 1944, this was about as state of the art as it could get. One entire wall seemed to be a transportable version of the Colossus computer from Bletchley Park; other machines seemed to be for monitoring radiation levels, electromagnetic fields, temperature and humidity. Yet more seemed to be concerned with seismic disturbance, weather forecasting and astronomical readings. More incongruous were the posters adorned with occult symbols, and the astrological charts and books on Celtic mysticism that were scattered across the work surfaces.

The entire place was alive with a relentless clicking of

rotors inside the machines, and the low electrical hum of transformers.

As his eyes adjusted to the low lighting condition inside the room, the Doctor became aware of several people looking at him, each of them in the same drab, brown coats that he was wearing.

The Doctor smiled at them. 'Hello. I'm Doctor… McGuinness. From St Andrew's University. I've been sent by the MoD as an observer of tonight's experiment. So here I am. Observing.' He removed the pencil from behind his ear and started scribbling furiously on the clipboard. 'Please, carry on. Don't mind me. Just pretend that I'm not here!'

Ignoring the bemused expressions of the other scientists, the Doctor busied himself at the controls of the Colossus, peering at the thin ribbon of paper that spewed relentlessly from the tickertape machine, and continuing to scrawl meaningless gobbledegook on his borrowed clipboard. He figured that he had a matter of minutes before one of the scientists started asking questions that he couldn't possibly answer, so he had to see what information he could glean as quickly as possible.

A memo with the letterhead of the Royal Observatory caught his eye, and he swiftly scanned its contents. It looked as though they had been trying to locate the origin of the mysterious radio transmission, but so far without success. 'Blast…' He tapped the pencil on his teeth. In another year or so they might have been able to use the radio telescope at Jodrell Bank, but for the moment...

'Excuse me?' He turned to face the scientists once more. 'Have any of you thought about reversing the polarity of the communications array that you have on the roof of this contraption and using the, admittedly primitive, RT equipment you have available to set up a narrow-band radio telescope to try and identify the source of the signal?'

The three scientists just stared at him blankly.

'No, I didn't think that you had.' The Doctor returned his attention to the Colossus. 'I suppose I could put in a call to Cowbridge House at Malmesbury, see if the guys and gals at the radar shadow factory can knock me up something that'll do the job. They owe me a favour for fixing their central-heating boiler during the winter of '39.'

'I'm not sure you should know about that top-secret facility,' came a stern voice from the doorway. 'And I'm certain that you shouldn't be wandering about in this one.'

The Doctor turned to see Sergeant Hughes standing the doorway of the truck, his pistol drawn.

'Outside.'

The Doctor stepped down from the truck into the now steady rain. Facing him was a row of soldiers, their rifles raised. Charlie Bevan was standing to one side, hands clasped behind the back of his head. The Doctor was directed to stand alongside him and was quickly frisked by one of the soldiers.

Charlie gave him an apologetic look. 'I guess that neither of us was fooling anybody.'

The Doctor didn't reply, but his expression darkened dangerously as the soldier removed the sonic screwdriver from his jacket pocket and handed it to Sergeant Hughes.

'Who the devil are these men, Sergeant?'

Professor Clearfield was making his way across the field towards them, his wet hair plastered to his head, his shoes and trouser-bottoms caked with mud.

'No idea, sir. This one claims to be the local police constable…'

'That's not the local plod,' said Private Stanford, firmly. 'Constable Sharples is helping with the evacuation. Left for Chippenham hours ago.'

'And him?' Clearfield peered at the Doctor suspiciously through his spectacles.

'No idea, sir. Says he's a Doctor...'

Really?' Clearfield snorted. 'You'd think the Germans would give their spies better cover stories.'

'He had this.' Hughes handed him the sonic screwdriver.

Clearfield turned it over in his hands, his brow furrowing as he examined it. As he did so it snapped open, the tip glowing bright green. He looked up at the Doctor with a puzzled frown. 'What is the function of this device?'

'It's an idiot detector. It lights up in the presence of

people who are tampering with things that they don't understand.'

There was a ripple of laughter from the assembled soldiers. Clearfield snapped the screwdriver closed and pushed it into his jacket pocket. 'I haven't got time for this nonsense. We're running behind schedule as it is. Sergeant, lock these two up somewhere secure. I'll question them properly later.'

'Sir.' The sergeant turned to two of the waiting solders. 'Rymill. Green. I want these two where I can see them. Put them in the back of the truck. And keep an eye on them!'

Grabbing the Doctor and Constable Bevan by the arms the soldiers marched them away down the path to where the truck that had delivered the Bell was parked.

'Sanford, you'd better check that there are no more unauthorised personnel in the area.'

'Even if there are, they're going to be too late.' Clearfield eyes blazed in anticipation. 'We switch on power to the Bell in ten minutes.'

From the back of the truck where he and Charlie were being held, the Doctor watched as the activity around the stone circle became more and more frantic as the equinox approached. He glanced at his watch. Just a few minutes to go.

Whilst outwardly calm, inside he was kicking himself. He had meant this to be nothing more than a quick fact-finding expedition, in and out before anyone even noticed they were there. Now his sonic screwdriver was in the hands of a scientist who was more than capable of deducing its function, and there was a fair chance that it would end up in the possession of the British Army.

Except…

If Robin's recollection of the events that were about to unfold were accurate, then everyone was about to be massacred by whatever the Bell brought through. Everyone except Robin Sanford.

And, if Charlie Bevan was correct, Professor Clearfield.

He checked his watch again. Whatever had happened here, they would know in less than four minutes.

In the control vehicle, Professor Clearfield watched the clock on the wall as the second hand ticked slowly around the dial.

'Prepare to transfer phase one power on my mark… Mark.'

The entire vehicle vibrated as a low, throbbing hum started to build. On dials all around the control room, needles started to rise.

'Stand by for phase two power on my mark…' Clearfield had to raise his voice to be heard now. 'Mark!'

The hum became a scream. Scrambling from his seat Clearfield pushed his way out of the door. 'Continue with phase three power. I have to see…'

In the field next to the stone circle the Bell was throbbing with energy, the grilles at its base sending flickering shafts of vivid, purple light dancing across the wet grass. The glistening ceramic shell began to steam as the rain boiled away, and the air was heavy with the smell of ozone.

The hairs on Clearfield's neck were standing on end, but it had nothing to do with the static being created by the machine. In the centre of the stone circle, a glow was beginning to build. 'It's working… he murmured. 'It's working.'

The low crump of anti-aircraft guns suddenly echoed from somewhere in the distance, and Clearfield glanced up in alarm. Above the treeline he could see the glow in the night sky that marked the position of the decoy site on Salisbury Plain. He glanced over at Sergeant Hughes for reassurance, but the soldier was transfixed by what was going on inside the circle.

The swirling Celtic patterns that decorated the stones had started to glow with a brilliant, electric-blue light. As the brightness increased it almost seemed as if the lines were dancing across the surface of the stone.

One of the scientists called out from the control vehicle. 'Full power achieved and holding!'

Clearfield held his breath. Only a few more seconds until the equinox…

With a sound like a thousand church bells chiming in unison, the centre of the circle erupted into a ball of brilliant light. With a cry, Clearfield turned away, shielding his eyes from the glare. From all around he could hear yelps of pain and the sound of shattering glass.

THE CRAWLING TERROR

There was sudden, deafening silence, and for a moment Clearfield wondered if his eardrums had burst.

He forced his streaming eyes open, desperate to see what the result of his experiment had been. The Bell was dark and silent, the purple glow extinguished, the ceramic surface steaming gently. The circle too was dark, but in the shadows at its centre something huge and black was gently moving to and fro.

Rubbing at his eyes, Clearfield started to edge forward, his heart pounding. All around the circle the soldiers were starting to move forward as well, rifles clutched nervously in their hands.

As one of them reached the edge of the circle, a huge claw reached out from the darkness, snatching him off his feet and snapping him almost in two.

Clearfield staggered backwards in terror as a vast, black scorpion burst out of the circle.

Chapter

Fourteen

From the back of the truck where he and the Doctor were being held, Charlie Bevan stared in horror as the huge scorpion emerged from the circle, its razor-sharp claws lashing out at the soldiers and scientists. There was a moment of stunned silence and then the night air erupted with the sound of gunfire.

'What is it?' Charlie's voice was hoarse with sheer terror.

The Doctor's face was grim. 'A Wyrrester.'

'A what?'

'A Wyrrester. A mutant arachnid species from the planet Typholchaktas in the Furey-King Maelstrom. Intelligent, vicious, dangerous.'

He turned to the two soldiers watching open-mouthed at the battle unfolding before them.

'Shouldn't you two be out there trying to stop it?'

The soldiers exchanged a brief glance, obviously unsure as to whether to leave their prisoners unguarded or not.

'Your colleagues are being massacred!' snapped the Doctor.

The two soldiers scrambled out of the truck, unshouldering their rifles as they ran towards the screeching monster.

The Doctor nodded in satisfaction and rose to his feet. 'Well, that avoids the need to come up with a complicated and longwinded escape plan.'

'Are they going to be able to stop it?' Charlie watched as the two young men – no more than boys, really – launched themselves into the fray.

'No,' said the Doctor bluntly. 'You heard the story that Robin told us.'

'So you just sent those men to their deaths.'

'Those men are already dead,' said the Doctor matter-of-factly. 'As far as you and I are concerned, they've been dead for seventy years. Nothing we do here will or can change that.'

'So that's it? We just leave them to it and go home?'

'Not before I retrieve my sonic screwdriver,' said the Doctor, jumping down from the back of the truck. 'Wait here.'

Charlie was suddenly very frightened; not least by the man who had whisked him back through time. All that he wanted to do was get as far away from him as possible, but as he watched the Doctor making his way across the green he knew that he had no choice but to do as he was told if he was going to escape from this nightmare.

*

Clearfield stumbled away from the circle, terrified at what he had unleashed. If he could get to the control vehicle, somehow reverse the settings of the Bell…

He was sent sprawling as something sharp hit him hard between the shoulder blades, and he was suddenly aware of a terrible burning sensation. Screaming with pain he tried to rise, but something held him fast, pinning him to the ground.

The wave of fire spread through his body until he was aware of nothing else. Finally, mercifully, the sensation started to recede, and the stinging weight pressing on his spine lifted.

Groaning with the effort, Clearfield rolled over onto his back, and came face to face with the monster that he had summoned into existence.

Despite the pain, the scientist in him couldn't help but be fascinated. Whilst at first glance the creature bore remarkable resemblance to a terrestrial scorpion, up close the differences became terrifyingly apparent. The face that loomed over him was not that of a simple animal, but instead blazed with a fierce, alien intelligence. The jet-black eyes seemed to look into his very soul, and mandibles quivered as the creature uttered harsh, indecipherable alien words.

Curling high over the thing's back, the needle-like sting at the tip of the tail still dripped with venom, and the two huge claws – inscribed, he realised, with the same swirling patterns as the stones – opened and closed slowly as the creature scrutinised him.

There was a fusillade of rifle shots, and bullets ricocheted off the scorpion's carapace. It scuttled around to face the oncoming soldiers, hissing with displeasure. Claws whipped out, sending men tumbling, arms, legs and even heads severed by the force of the blows.

As the monster pursued its attackers across the field, Clearfield was suddenly aware of a figure approaching though the rain. As he tried to focus, he realised that it was the man that they had caught in the control room earlier. What was it that he had called himself?

'Doctor…' he spluttered as the man hunched down on the grass beside him. 'I think this house call might be a little late…'

The Doctor said nothing, just reached out and removed the silver tube that nestled in Clearfield's jacket pocket.

'Ah,' said the professor weakly. 'I see.'

The Doctor snapped open the device and it warbled faintly as he ran it over the professor's head and torso.

'Well? Does it still say that I'm an idiot?'

The Doctor examined the readings on the device. 'Your system has been flooded with a powerful alien neurotoxin that is reacting with the residual energy field left over from the activation of the Bell.'

'What does that mean?' asked Clearfield, coughing as tremors started to wrack his body. 'What will that do to me?'

'I don't know.' The Doctor got to his feet. 'I guess that you can tell me in seventy years' time.'

'Wait…' Clearfield reached out feebly, already unable

to feel any sensation in his fingers. 'You're not just going to leave me here?'

'I'm sorry,' said the Doctor, slipping the device into his own jacket pocket. 'There's nothing that I'm able to do.'

Then he turned and walked slowly away.

Privates Sanford and Davies had been patrolling the perimeter of the village checking for more intruders when the Bell activated. The shock wave had practically knocked them off their feet, and the flash had lit up the surrounding countryside for miles. So much for their decoy site...

Sanford's head was still ringing with the noise. He grinned at the other man. 'I guess that's why they call it the Bell.'

The two of them started to make their way back through the village when the sound of gunshots rang out through the damp night air. Then the sound of screaming.

And then the sound of something else...

'What in the name of God was that?' Sanford's skin went cold as the blood-curdling, inhuman screech echoed through the night air.

'Well, we're not going to find out hanging about here.' Private Davies unslung his Lee Enfield rifle from his shoulder and pulled back the bolt. 'Come on!'

He ran off through the rain.

'No, Davies, wait.' Cursing, Sanford unshouldered his own rifle and started to run after him. As he did so a sudden stabbing pain stopped him dead in his tracks. He clutched at his chest as the familiar tightening sensation took hold.

'Oh, please, no.'

Dropping his rifle he scrabbled in his uniform pocket for the bottle of pills that he had carried with him every day since he was a child.

'Not now.'

As he struggled to unscrew the top from the little glass bottle he suddenly heard someone trying to hide in the shadows ahead of him.

The pill bottle slipped from his fingers, scattering its contents on the wet earth as he scrabbled to pick up his rifle.

'Halt!' he stammered. 'Who goes there?'

A figure emerged from the garden of one of the cottages at the edge of the green, his hands raised. It was one of spies that they had caught earlier!

'How did you get away? And what's going on back there? Your friends come to rescue you, have they?'

The man dressed like a policeman shook his head, obviously scared witless by something. 'No. Don't shoot! It's not me you need to worry about – it's the thing. The scorpion!'

'Scorpion?' Sanford struggled to concentrate. He could feel his forehead going clammy as his heart started to pound faster and faster, threatening to burst from his chest. 'What are you talking about?' He wiped the sweat from his eyes with his sleeve. His vision was starting to blur at the edges. 'And where's your mate?'

'Here.'

The other man, the tall, strange-looking one, had suddenly appeared from nowhere. Private Sanford swung his rifle to cover him.

'Private, you need to listen to me.' The man's voice was compelling, hypnotic. 'This experiment, this Bell, was a horrible, dangerous mistake. It has brought something onto this world, a creature that, if unchecked, will destroy every living thing.'

'Creature? What do you mean, creature?'

'An alien. A being from another planet. At the moment it's alone, but soon there will be more. Hundreds more. And only you can stop it.'

'Me?'

From the direction of the stone circle, Sanford could see flames now, and hear the unmistakable rattle of a Sten gun. The high-pitched animalistic scream came again followed by the dull crump of a hand grenade.

As the explosion lit up the night sky, Sanford caught a glimpse of a monstrous silhouette.

'Dear God…' He let his rifle drop.

'This thing cannot be stopped with bullets, Private.' The tall man's voice cut through the cacophony. 'But it can be destroyed. You can destroy it…'

He bent down, scooping the spilt pills back into their bottle and screwing the cap back on.

'Oh yeah?' Sanford gave an almost hysterical laugh. 'Me and whose army?'

The man tossed the bottle to him. 'Actually, you and the Luftwaffe…'

That simple sentence struck home with almost physical force.

The man was right. The carbon arc searchlight was still sitting in front of them on the village green. If the German aircraft were still in the area then he had the means to show them exactly where to drop their bombs.

'The arc light…' He motioned at the two men with his rifle. 'Right. Turn around.'

The tall man shook his head, his face in shadow. 'This is for you to do. I've already given all the help that I dare. We cannot, *must* not, get involved any further.'

Sanford raised his rifle. 'I said, turn around.'

The policeman couldn't tear his gaze from the barrel of the rifle. Then, with a deep sigh of resignation, the tall man closed his eyes.

'Soldiers…'

Keeping the two men covered, Sanford shook two of his pills into the palm of his hand, almost choking as he struggled to swallow them dry. Trying to slow his breathing and calm his hammering heart, Sanford marched the two prisoners across the green, keeping them to the shadows, his eyes never wavering from the monstrous shape that heaved and roared in the centre of the stone circle.

Even from here he could see that the field around the circle was littered with bodies. It had taken this creature less than ten minutes to massacre an entire battalion, and they hadn't even slowed it down.

As he watched, the creature swung around and lumbered across to where the Bell was standing. The squat grey shape was still steaming in the damp March air. As the creature drew near it started to stab at the controls on the casing with its claws, snipping cables and reconnecting them with surprising dexterity.

Then, to Sanford's horror, the base of the Bell started to glow with unearthly purple light, and the low, throbbing hum started to build once more, making the ground beneath his feet vibrate. The creature had tapped into some other power source. It was reactivating the machine.

'You're running out of time, Private Sanford,' said the tall man. 'It's calling for reinforcements! You need to get that light on!'

'Shut your neck,' he snapped. But the man was right. He was out of time. 'Right you two, we're going to get to that searchlight and start that generator. Quickly now! Whilst that thing is busy!'

Wincing with the pain that was building in his chest once more, Sanford urged the two prisoners forward. The tightness in his chest was now almost unbearable, and his vision was beginning to blur. 'You,' he pointed at the policeman. 'Start it.'

Eyes fixed on the rifle, the policeman gripped the handle, his face flushing as he tried to turn the stiff crank. The generator gave a click but nothing more.

'Again!'

Sweating with the effort, the policeman turned the handle again, this time coaxing a choking cough from the engine.

'Again!'

Sanford offered a prayer of relief as finally, on the third turn, the generator roared into life.

He staggered across to the searchlight, throwing the switch and shielding his eyes as the arc spat and spluttered into life. A beam of brilliant light lanced up into the cloud-filled sky. Clawing his way around to the controls on the other side, he unlocked the searchlight and twisted the wheel, bringing that beam to bear on the creature in front of him.

The powerful searchlight raked across the village green, lighting up the tableau in the field as if it was a stage production. Caught in the glare, the monstrous scorpion staggered backward from where it was working on the Bell, hissing with pain as its eyes were scorched by the brilliance of the light.

Sanford gave a gasp of disbelief as the searchlight finally revealed the full horror of the thing that had killed his friends and colleagues, and he felt his chest tighten even further.

Claws snapping in anger, the creature scuttled around trying to locate the source of the light that was blinding it. As it did so, it gave a bellow of rage and, to Sanford's horror, started to make its way down the path towards him.

Sanford stepped back from the searchlight, fumbling

with his rifle, realising that his prisoners had taken advantage of the distraction and had fled, vanishing into the rain.

As the scorpion bore down on him Sanford abandoned the searchlight and started to run towards the church. If he could just get to the cellar… His legs felt as though they were made from lead, and there was a droning hum beginning to build in his head.

He had almost reached the churchyard when his ailing heart finally got the better of him and his legs gave out. With a cry of despair Sanford collapsed onto the wet grass of the village green. As he lay there, feeling the cool patter of rain on his face, it suddenly struck him that the droning noise wasn't in his head after all. It was coming from the sky.

Moments later all he could hear was the roar of high explosives, and the screams of the monstrous scorpion, as the Luftwaffe found their target.

Charlie Bevan ran. Ahead of him the Doctor was a thin, gangly shadow, flitting through the rain. Behind them the village green had erupted into a blaze of light and noise as the German bombs started to fall.

They raced up the footpath towards the circle. The ground underfoot was slick with rain and blood and, as they dodged through the bodies that littered the grass, Charlie suddenly slipped, crashing heavily to the ground.

'Doctor!' he screamed, terrified of being left behind. Skidding to a halt, the Doctor ran back to him, grasping him by the collar and hauling him to his feet. As he did so there was a whistling shriek, and something huge and grey plummeted from the sky, landing in the centre of the circle just yards from them.

The impact threw both men to the floor and Charlie threw his hands over his head, waiting for the explosion that would end his life.

It didn't come.

He felt hands pulling him upright once more.

'Don't just lie there, man!' yelled the Doctor angrily. 'Keep going!'

As the explosions started up once more, the two of them ran for their lives. Behind them flames billowed hundreds of feet into the cold night air. For what seemed like an eternity there was nothing but noise and light, but finally the chaos was left behind and the two of them reached the meadow where the TARDIS had landed.

Unlocking the doors, the Doctor bundled Charlie inside. Moments later there was a swirl of wind, and a grating rasp as the TARDIS faded from the fields of Ringstone.

Through the trees, in the village, the air raid slowly started to subside, and soon there was nothing but the low crackle of distant fires and the distant, lonesome tolling of a church bell sounding the all-clear.

Chapter

Fifteen

'So, the British experiment ended in disaster. That still doesn't explain why you have this?' Clara nodded towards the Bell with its swastika markings, waiting for an explanation.

'The German bombs completely destroyed the British machine,' Clearfield told her. 'The Bell, the control assemblies, the research notes, everything. Starting again would have taken years, and the end of the war put paid to any thought of that. But the German device had never been used as intended. The German Bell was still out there!'

'So you tracked it down.' Clara wracked her memory. 'Didn't a lot of Nazi war criminals escape to South America? Paraguay, Argentina, places like that?'

Clearfield nodded. 'And I spent a lot of time in those countries, finding people who had been close to the project, trying to learn what had become of the Nazi Bell. In the end I learnt that both it and SS General Kammler had been removed from the test facility in

Poland by U-boat, and taken to a secret submarine base in Neuschwabenland.'

Clara shrugged, unfamiliar with the word.

'The Antarctic.'

She frowned. 'But this must have cost a fortune. Finding the Bell, transporting back here, setting up this facility. Where are you getting the money?'

Clearfield gave a sly smile. 'There are still plenty of people who would like to see the Nazi empire rise again. People with access to the money that they stockpiled at the end of the war.'

'So you're financing the recreation of the Bell experiments using Nazi gold.'

'Yes.'

'And you returned here to set up in the same place again. Using the circle.'

'I had hoped to.' He sighed. 'Sadly the damage to the stone circle was so great that the energies it created are no longer available to control the Bell properly.'

'Hence this.' Clara indicated the black monoliths, the spirals on the screens still swirling in endless complex patterns. 'But surely there are dozens, if not hundreds of stone circles like this scattered around the countryside. Surely you could just relocate to one of them?'

Clearfield shook his head. 'There are very few with the particular properties that made the one here in Ringstone so special. Our ancestors understood the special nature of the stones; modern man just sees them as curiosities of a bygone age. Most of the circles of power have been destroyed by farmers anxious to use the fields to grow crops… They call it progress.'

'OK.' Clara crossed her arms. 'You recover a Nazi machine that's remained hidden since the war, you manage to fund the creation of a high-tech stone circle, and you breed giant insects. So here's the million-dollar question. What is it all for?'

Clearfield leaned forward urgently. 'The Wyrresters that tried to open a portal here in the war are the same ones that I am working with now. They are pariahs from their own species, hunted, persecuted… Looking for refuge. I had hoped to create a digital version of the circle, a means of opening the portal artificially, but…' He sighed. 'The energies of ley lines require very specific conditions. My experiments have only been partially successful. I cannot enable a physical transference, only a mental one.'

'Hence the insects.' Clara glanced at the vile shapes crawling in the cages on the far side of the laboratory. 'You've created bodies for them!'

Clearfield nodded. 'I have been experimenting for years, trying to find a form that will allow them to survive here on Earth. The creatures that you have seen, the spiders, the crane flies, they were just tests, trials to see if the Wyrresters could inhabit and control those bodies… Those tests were not entirely successful.'

Clara was horrified. 'So those insects have alien minds?'

'Partially. Those early experiments have a shared mind, a shared consciousness, but the Wyrrester part is unable to dominate totally, sometimes the animal gains the upper hand. When it does, the creatures revert to their basic nature... Ultimately it leads to madness, then death. They have served their purpose, though, as guards, as distractions whilst we prepare the final phase.'

'That's horrible. Horrible.' Clara looked at him with disgust. 'Did the Wyrresters that you persuaded to go through with this... procedure know they were just... test subjects?'

'The Wyrresters who agreed to those experiments were totally committed to their cause,' said Clearfield coldly. 'If our tests with human subjects had been as successful...'

'You tried to do this with people?'

Of course!' Clearfield looked at her as if it was the most natural thing in the world. 'If the Wyrrester mind was capable of being grafted into a human form then that would have been the most suitable solution. Unfortunately the human mind is not compatible.'

'*Or so we had thought!*'

'I'm sorry?' Clearfield looked up as the hissing voice rang out once more. 'You said that it *was* impossible. That you *could* not inhabit a human mind!'

'*That was true. But this girl is different. Her mind is something that we have not encountered before. Her neural pathways have been opened by technology that is not of this planet. She will be receptive to us. Place her in the circle.*'

'What? No!'

'*Do as you are instructed, Clearfield!*'

'But, Gebbron, the hybrid insect bodies that I've created for you are an unqualified success. All the work that I have done…'

'You have had years, and yet still there are problems! The creatures that you have engineered still remain primitive. This girl provides a new opportunity. I will not squander it. You need my guidance, and now we have the means for me to provide it. She will be my vessel.'

Clara looked up in alarm. 'Erm, now hang on a minute… Not sure I'm keen on being a vessel…'

'Do as we say!'

Clearfield looked utterly dejected. 'You leave me no choice.'

Clara waved a hand nervously. 'Hello... Like I said… Not keen!'

Clearfield reached into his jacket and withdrew his revolver. 'I'm sorry, Clara. I… you… must do what Gebbron asks.' He gestured to the circle. 'Stand in the centre.'

Clara didn't move.

Clearfield's tone hardened. 'The process will work just as well if you are unconscious, Miss Oswald.'

The threat was quite clear. Realising she had no choice, Clara stepped into the circle of black obelisks.

Clearfield slipped into a seat in front of one of the many control consoles and started snapping on switches. Slowly a low throb of power started to build and the base of the Bell started to glow with a deep purple light.

*

'Sir!'

Captain Wilson looked up as the private in charge of the monitoring communications station stepped into the command vehicle.

'Positive confirmation of energy signature from the site, sir. Very weak, but definitely the wavelengths that you told us to look for.'

Wilson cast a worried look at his commanding officer. Colonel Dickinson's face remained impassive, but something about his manner, the way that he held himself, abruptly changed and he suddenly seemed a lot older, a lot wearier.

As Dickinson reached for the phone to issue the order that would wipe Ringstone from the map, Wilson pulled himself from his chair.

'Sir, a moment.'

Dickinson's hand hesitated on the receiver. 'What is it, Captain?'

'Permission to lead a small team inside the perimeter, sir.'

'To what end?'

'Locate the Bell, disable or destroy it, evacuate as many civilians as possible.'

The colonel regarded him closely, his hand still resting on the telephone handset. 'And the hostiles?'

'We've armour-piercing rounds available, and two of the Next-generation Light Anti-tank Weapons. Plus eight gallons of the experimental pesticide. If all that fails, then we'll just blow the wretched things up with grenades.'

The colonel said nothing.

'Give me two hours,' said the captain softly. 'All the intelligence points to the fact that whoever is operating the device will wait until the vernal equinox before activating at full power. Give me two hours before you call in that air strike.'

Dickinson removed his hand from the telephone. 'All right, Captain. But, if I see that energy signature start to spike, I'm pulling you and your team out and making that call.'

Wilson saluted. 'Sir.'

As the captain turned to leave, Dickinson called after him. 'Captain Wilson…'

'Sir?'

'Good luck.'

The two men held each other's gaze for a moment, both of them aware of what was at stake. Then Captain Wilson hurried off to assemble his squad.

'Uh, oh.'

The Doctor peered at a readout on the TARDIS console that had suddenly flickered into life.

"What is it?' Charlie Bevan looked up in alarm.

'An energy reading. From your time. The Bell has just been activated.'

'But I thought that you said that we had until the… the vernal equinox?'

'I did.' The Doctor darted around the console, adjusting controls. 'This is something different.' He frowned. 'And it's not coming from the circle, its coming from the science park.'

'Clearfield?'

'Who else?' The Doctor slammed down the materialisation control. 'I think it's time we found out exactly how our professor survived, and why he is determined to start everything up again.'

The grating, rasping roar of the TARDIS engines reverberated around the console room, and the huge, spinning rotors started to slow down. The Doctor was across the control room and out of the doors before they had even stopped moving. Charlie hurried after him.

Charlie emerged into brilliant sunlight. The TARDIS had landed in the car park of the industrial estate, nestled against the wall of one of the large prefabricated buildings. The Doctor was already over at the doors, using his sonic screwdriver to break in.

The glass doors slid open with a hiss and the Doctor vanished inside. Pulling the TARDIS doors closed, Charlie ran to catch up with him.

The interior of the building was dark and deserted, but there was a low electrical hum that made all the doors and windows rattle faintly. It was setting Charlie's teeth on edge.

As they made their way slowly down the wide corridor that led from the main reception area they suddenly heard a noise, a banging accompanied by a muffled voice. 'That sounds like Angela,' said Charlie, listening to the distant cries for help.

They followed the noise to a locked cupboard at the end of a corridor leading off the main walkway. The Doctor pressed his sonic screwdriver to the lock, and there was a clatter of tumblers as it released. Immediately the door slammed open and a frantic figure burst from the cupboard, screaming and lashing out with her fists.

The Doctor dodged out of the way in time, but Charlie was too slow, catching a blow on the side of the head as Angela tried to push her way past them.

'Hey! It's us!' he yelped.

The young vet skidded to a halt. 'Oh, thank God!' Her relief was palpable. 'I thought that you were Clearfield's zombies coming back.'

'Where's Clara?' asked the Doctor sharply.

'He's got her through there.' Angela pointed at the wide double-doors at the end of the corridor.

Jaw clenched, the Doctor spun on his heel and set off towards them.

'Be careful, Doctor!' Angela called after him. 'He's got a gun.'

Disregarding her warning, the Doctor threw the doors open and marched brazenly into the room beyond. Charlie and Angela followed him cautiously. The noise from inside the room swamped all other sounds, a low throbbing that Charlie could feel through the floor. Purple light blazed from the centre of the room sending shadows dancing across the walls. A circle of thirteen monolithic black shapes dominated the middle of the room, each one crackling with energy.

In their centre stood Clara.

The Doctor raised his sonic screwdriver. 'Clearfield!' he shouted. 'Turn it off! Now!'

The heads of everyone in the room snapped around to look at him.

Clearfield had risen from his seat and was staring at the Doctor in disbelief. 'You…'

'I mean it,' said the Doctor dangerously. 'Either you turn it off now, or I will.'

Clearfield reached out and pressed a series of switches. Slowly the light from the Bell and the noise of the machinery faded. Harsh fluorescent lights snapped on. Technicians at the other consoles started to rise, but Clearfield motioned to them to stay where they were. Slowly he walked across the room towards the Doctor.

'Well, well, well… The Doctor and his idiot detector. You said that we would meet in seventy years and here you are. I love a man of his word.'

The Doctor ignored him. 'Are you all right, Clara?'

For a moment she said nothing, then nodded her head weakly.

Clearfield was now a few feet from the Doctor, regarding him with a professional curiosity. 'Extraordinary. Seventy years since I last set eyes on you, and yet you haven't changed at all.'

'I could say the same.' The Doctor studied the mask that covered one half of Clearfield's face. 'Apart from that, of course.'

'This?' Clearfield raised a hand to touch the translucent

plastic. 'Let me tell you about this. This is a constant reminder of a night in 1944, of a night where I tried to contact another world.' His voice stared to crack as emotion started to get the better of him. 'This is a reminder of a plea I made to a man for help. A man who said that he could not, *would not* help.' His voice was shaking with anger now. 'This is a constant reminder of you!'

He peeled the mask away from his head, and the room echoed to Angela's scream of horror.

Chapter

Sixteen

The Doctor stared sadly at the ravaged face that lay underneath the mask. There was virtually nothing left of the left side of Clearfield's head, just bone and a fused mass of scar tissue. He held the gaze of Clearfield's remaining eye. 'I'm sorry.'

'He's sorry…' Clearfield gave a barking, humourless laugh and pulled the plastic mask back into place. 'Seventy years of seeing this face in the mirror every day, and he says he's sorry.'

'It was already a part of history. What happened that night…'

'Let me tell you exactly what happened that night!' spat Clearfield. 'You were quite right: the combination of Wyrrester venom and the residual mutagenic field generated by the Bell did combine in an unusual way. It made me invulnerable, strong, boosted my capacity to learn, made me practically immortal!' He took a deep breath. 'It should have been my greatest moment, my apotheosis!'

He glared at the Doctor. 'I had only managed to crawl a couple of yards from where you left me when the bombs began to fall. If you had helped me get clear then I would have survived unscathed, as it was…' He closed his eyes, reliving the moment. 'I took shelter underneath the control vehicle, unfortunately a bomb landed close alongside, rupturing the fuel tank. I was trapped when the flames took hold. I should have died, but the Wyrrester's venom prevented that. When the flames subsided I crawled from the wreckage a… *changed* man. I have not aged a day since then.'

'And this?' The Doctor gestured to the machines, the circle.

'This is the work of a lifetime…'

'The mistake of a lifetime.' The Doctor stepped forward, intending to reason with him. 'The Wyrresters…'

'The Wyrresters are the greatest boon that man could wish for. Their voices have been inside my head for most of my entire adult life.' Clearfield pulled the pistol from inside his jacket. 'I intend to help them in their desire to create a colony here on Earth and I am not going to let you stand in my way.'

He levelled the gun at the Doctor's head.

Kevin Alperton was in the kitchen of Robin Sanford's house, cleaning up the broken glass, and helping the old man nail a sheet of timber across the window, when he noticed the movement in the field outside.

His first thought was that yet another type of insect

was going to attack, but as he looked closer he realised that the movement came from four soldiers making their way through the field behind the house.

'Mr Sanford!' he called out. 'Look!'

Robin Sanford joined him at the window. 'About bloomin' time!' He opened the back door, taking a large key from a hook and handing it to Kevin. 'Go and unlock the gate at the end of the garden. They'll make one devil of a racket if they try and climb over.'

Kevin took the key nervously. 'Outside?'

'Sure. I'll cover you from the window.' Robin hefted the shotgun. 'Well, go on!'

Heart pounding, Kevin stepped out into well-kept patio garden. The gate at the far end was probably only about fifteen feet away, but it suddenly looked like a mile. Gripping the key tightly, he started to pick his way slowly down the garden, making sure that his shoes made as little sound as possible on the stone slabs.

The garden was a tangle of plants in pots, interspersed with plastic chairs and bird feeders. Kevin was just grateful that Mr Sanford liked patios instead of lawns. He was still struggling to forget the image of the fox struggling wildly on his own lawn the previous night. At least the insects couldn't burrow through stone.

He was almost at the gate when a tall shape almost hidden by foliage caught his eye. There was something familiar about it…

Curiosity overcoming his fear he pulled aside the leaves. It was a stone, about four feet high, covered with moss and lichen. Kevin could see swirls and patterns carved in the rock.

There was a hiss from behind him that made Kevin jump. Mr Sanford was glaring at him from the window. 'What are you dithering for? Get that gate open!'

Hurrying forward, Kevin fumbled with the big clunky padlock, painfully aware of the noise that he was making as he did so. The lock opened with a click and Kevin opened the wooden gate.

He found himself staring down the barrel of a gun.

'Hold up,' came a gruff voice. 'It's just a kid.'

Four heavily armed soldiers pushed past him into the garden, methodically checking each corner and patch of shadow until they were certain that the area was secure.

Kevin could see that two of the soldiers had their rifles aimed at the kitchen window where the barrel of Mr Sanford's shotgun was clearly visible.

'Lower the weapon please, sir,' barked one of them.

There was a clink of broken glass as the gun barrel was withdrawn through the broken window, and a muffled voice came from inside the house. 'I'm on your damn side, you know.'

The soldiers hustled Kevin towards the back door and they all bundled inside.

'Arnopp, Palmer, check the front. Hawkins, upstairs.' One of the soldiers, obviously the leader, removed his helmet. 'I'm Captain Wilson. Is there anyone else in the house?'

Robin Sanford shook his head. 'Just me and the boy.'

'And you are?'

'Sanford. Robin Sanford. This is Kevin.'

'Alperton.' Kevin added. 'My last name's Alperton.'

'What about earlier? The two on the bike. Who are they?'

Robin raised an eyebrow. 'You saw that, eh? Then I guess that it's you that we have to thank for taking pot shots at that spider.'

Wilson nodded. 'Always happy to help. Now, those other two…'

'It was Constable Bevan,' piped up Kevin. And the Doctor.'

'The doctor? Who's he? Local GP?'

'Don't really know,' said Robin gruffly. 'Scientist of some kind.'

Wilson exchanged a glance with one of his men. 'Mr Sanford. I gather that you were stationed here during the war…'

'That's right. Home Guard. Would have signed up but I have problems with my chest, see…'

'Sir, I need you to tell me everything that you can about "Project Big Ben".'

Robin Sanford stiffened. 'What do you know about that?'

'We have reason to think that someone is trying to recreate those experiments.'

'No!' Robin shook his head angrily. 'No, that's impossible!'

'Sir, our instruments are picking up a very distinctive

energy signature from somewhere in this vicinity. Someone is operating a Bell device and I need to find it and destroy it!' Wilson gestured to one of the chairs. 'Sit down. Please.'

Robin hesitated, but Wilson's expression made it quite clear that he was in no mood for games.

'Please.'

Robin sat.

Placing his helmet on the kitchen table, Captain Wilson pulled over a chair and sat facing him. 'Now, I need you to tell me everything that you know about this machine. And this mysterious Doctor.'

As Clearfield levelled the service revolver at the Doctor's forehead, there was a sudden hissing scream, and the crash of metal as all the cages against the far wall of the building opened. At once an angry tide of snapping insects surged across the floor.

Moments later the lights went out, plunging the entire building into total darkness.

'Doctor! Run!' shouted Charlie Bevan.

The Doctor needed no encouragement. As he threw himself to one side there was a deafening explosion as Clearfield's gun went off. In the brilliant glare of the muzzle flash, the Doctor could see Clara standing stock still in the centre of the techno-circle as huge insects swarmed round her.

The gun fired again, and the Doctor used the momentary illumination to orient himself. Charlie and

Angela were pressed against the far wall, struggling to open one of the fire doors. Clara still hadn't moved.

As one of the hybrid insects scuttled towards him, the Doctor darted forward, kicking it out of the way and cannoning into Clearfield, knocking him off balance. As the professor crashed to the floor, the gun went off for a third time, the bullet ricocheting wildly around the metal walkways in the ceiling. Practically on his hands and knees, the Doctor scampered across the floor to the dark, hulking shape of the Bell. He could feel the hair on his arms stand on end with the static that still clung to its surface. Working quickly, and in near darkness, he located an access panel set into the base of the machine and slid it open.

A pale violet glow washed across his hands. The space inside the base of the Bell was packed with glass tubes, each one holding a glowing, purple liquid. The Doctor hesitated. With no time to make a proper study of the workings of the Bell, he had no idea which components would disable it effectively. More worrying, he had no idea which components might still hold a charge.

With time rapidly running out, he used the technique that had served him well in so many of his previous incarnations.

'Eeny, meeny, miny…'

He grasped hold of one of the glass tubes and pulled hard. Wires and pipes tore out of their sockets, and there was a shower of sparks as he wrenched it from its housing. 'Mo.'

Stuffing the tube inside his jacket pocket, the Doctor scrambled to his feet. He could still make out the vague shape of Clara in the centre of the circle. He hurried over to her side. 'Come on!'

Grabbing her by the hand, he raced across the darkened warehouse to where Charlie and Angela were waiting. As they ran, the double doors suddenly swung open and a shaft of light slashed across the floor. Skittering insects ran for cover as light flooded the room.

Barely slowing down, the Doctor hurtled out into the daylight, still half dragging Clara behind him. As Charlie and Angela both scrambled out after them, the Doctor released his grip on Clara's hand, slamming the doors closed behind them and pressing the tip of his sonic screwdriver to the lock. There was a hiss of steam, and a drop of molten metal oozed from the keyhole as the lock was fused into a sold mass.

Angela shot him a stern look. 'Locking fire doors is a breach of the Health and Safety at Work Act, you know.'

'So is letting pets loose in the workplace.' The Doctor grinned at her. 'Thanks very much for that, by the way!'

'What were those things?' Charlie was struggling to find a portion of his handkerchief not covered in mud, grease or slime.

'Vessels. Receptacles. Bodies for the Wyrresters.' The Doctor glanced at his watch. 'We've probably slowed them down, but not enough, not nearly enough…' He ushered them away from the building. 'We need to get back to the TARDIS. You three can use the bike to get back to Robin Sanford's house.'

'What are you going to do?' asked Charlie.

'I have to destroy that machine.'

Suddenly aware that Clara wasn't with them, the Doctor stopped and looked around for her. She was still standing outside the building, hands pressed to either side of her face. The Doctor hurried back to her side. 'Are you all right?'

Clara gave him a weak smile. 'Just a bit disorientated, that's all.'

The Doctor peered into her eyes worriedly. 'I'm not surprised, the energies in that room would be enough to upset the most robust constitution.' He squeezed her shoulder reassuringly. 'You're fine.'

The two of them hurried around the building to where Charlie and Angela were waiting in the shadow of the TARDIS. The Doctor unlocked the door and between them they managed to haul the Norton and sidecar out through the double doors. As they did so Angela glanced in through the open doors, and then abruptly stepped back, giving the Doctor a look that was half amazement, half pure terror.

'I'm sure that Constable Bevan will tell you everything that you need to know,' said the Doctor. He turned to Clara. 'You'd better drive. Charlie here has already caused enough damage as it is.'

'Hey!' Charlie looked at him indignantly.

Clara backed away, shaking her head. 'I don't think so…'

'All right…' The Doctor's eye's narrowed. 'Looks like it's you driving again after all, constable.'

Charlie clambered onto the bike, Angela swinging herself up onto the seat behind him.

The Doctor helped Clara into the sidecar. 'Are you sure that you are all right?'

'Honestly. I've just got a headache, that's all.'

The Doctor stepped back as Charlie kicked the big Norton into life. 'I'll meet you at the farmhouse later. Just lock the doors and stay inside.'

Charlie nodded and the Norton roared off through the car park. The Doctor watched as it vanished along the road, then carefully removed the glass vial from his jacket.

He held it up to the light, watching the thick, purple liquid churn and swirl inside the glass. 'Just a headache…' he murmured, then turned and stepped inside the TARDIS.

Clara opened her eyes. Everything around her was dark. She tried to open her mouth, but her tongue felt thick and heavy. She tried to move, but her limbs seemed sluggish, unresponsive.

Abruptly a glaring light snapped on, dazzling her, and she became aware of two shapes moving cautiously towards her through the brightness, one of them larger than the other.

'Remarkable. I had not expected consciousness to return so soon.'

'We have underestimated the abilities of these primitives. Perhaps we should reconsider our plan.'

With a chill of recognition, Clara realised that the low, bubbling voices were the same as the one she had heard speaking earlier. They were the voices of the aliens.

As she tried to peer through the brilliant haze, one of the shapes came closer, and she recoiled in horror as the light illuminated every tiny detail of the thing in front of her.

The creature was like a huge scorpion, about four metres long. Its black, shiny carapace was covered in sharp bristles, and it moved skittishly on six spindly legs. Two huge claws, their surfaces covered with swirling arcane symbols, opened and closed slowly, and a curved tail, tipped with a wicked looking barb, coiled and uncoiled agitatedly.

The creature leaned in, and Clara started to panic as it loomed over her. She tried to back away, but an invisible force held her firmly in place. Black, piercing eyes blazed in the folds of skin that made up the monster's face, and thick, fleshy mouthparts moved wetly as it examined her.

Clara raised her hands to ward it off, but as she did so she realised that it wasn't hands that she was raising, it was two black, chitinous claws, the edges razor sharp, their surface covered in whorls and patterns.

She froze, desperate to refute the evidence of her own eyes.

Her own eyes...

As the horror of what had happened to her struck

home she tried to scream, but the only sound that she could make was a vile, burbling cough.

The transference had been successful.

Her mind was in the body of a Wyrrester.

Chapter

Seventeen

'Sir, we've got civilians incoming.'

Captain Wilson hurried up the stairs to the front bedroom where Private Hawkins had set up his observation post. The window was open, and Hawkins had set up his big L115A3 sniper rifle so that he could cover the whole of the front yard.

At the far end of the narrow road that led towards the village, Wilson could see the bulky green shape of the Norton motorbike and sidecar. He could make out three figures clinging on desperately as it sped towards them.

Then he caught sight of the shapes in the sky behind them.

Hawkins spotted them as well, snatching up his rifle and taking careful aim. There was a deafening crack and one of the mosquitoes exploded in a cloud of legs, wings and bodily fluids.

'Good man!' Wilson clapped him on the shoulder. 'See if you can get any more of the buggers.'

He bounded down the stairs, taking them two at a

time. 'Arnopp, we need some of that A7E insecticide!' he bellowed. 'Palmer, watch the rear.'

He hauled open the front door as Private Arnopp hurried to join him, struggling with a large plastic container of clear liquid attached to an industrial spray head. Setting down the insecticide, the two men took up positions against the wall of the house as the motorbike screeched to a halt in front of them.

The rider and passengers barely had time to dismount before the air was filled with an angry buzzing and the mosquitoes swept into the farmyard.

Wilson and Arnopp both opened fire with their SA80s, the high-velocity ammunition tearing into the hovering insects. The three civilians raced across the yard, covering their heads with their arms as blood and ichor showered down around them.

'Inside! Inside!' shouted Wilson, swinging around and loosing off another burst of gunfire, as several of the insects swooped past his head.

The two women vanished in through the front door, but one of the mosquitoes lunged forward, hovering in front of the policeman and cutting off his escape route.

Wilson struggled to bring his gun to bear on the insect, but the panicked policeman was moving around too much.

'Arnopp, do you have a clean shot?' he yelled.

'No!'

The policeman let out a scream of terror as another of the insects swooped down, landing hard on his back.

Cursing, Wilson sprang to his feet, abandoning his assault rifle and snatching up the container of insecticide instead. He ran forwards, unleashing a torrent of spray that doused both the mosquitoes and the policeman.

The effect was instantaneous. The two insects sprang away from their victim as if they had been scalded. Wings soaked in the insecticide, they crashed to the floor, legs thrashing uncontrollably.

The policeman stumbled around blindly, desperately trying to clear the liquid from his eyes. Wilson grabbed him by the collar of his uniform and dragged him towards the house. As he did so, he heard the angry buzz of wings approaching from behind and something hit him between the shoulder blades.

Almost simultaneously there was a sharp, explosive crack from the upstairs window, and the shattered body of the mosquito dropped onto the cobblestones next to its dying brethren.

Repelled by the smell of the insecticide, or somehow aware that it faced insurmountable opposition, the remaining insect shot up into the air then vanished over the trees, its harsh buzzing slowly fading until there was silence once more.

Wilson gave a grateful thumbs-up to Private Hawkins, then turned to Corporal Palmer who was making his way cautiously from the house. 'Get the constable inside, would you, Palmer? Make sure he sluices that stuff off him with plenty of cold water. The boffins say that it's harmless to humans, but better safe than sorry, eh?'

'Sir.' The corporal led the spluttering policeman inside the house.

Snatching up his discarded rifle, Captain Wilson regarded the motorbike and sidecar with satisfaction.

He turned to Arnopp with a smile. 'Looks like we have motorised transport.'

In the cool calm of the TARDIS interior, the Doctor stood hunched over one of the diagnostic consoles that bordered the control room, peering worriedly at the readout on a screen.

A blackboard standing next to him was covered with complex calculations scrawled in chalk. As far as the Doctor could ascertain, the Bell had just operated in a way that was secondary to its main purpose. Energy emissions had certainly been sent to, and received from, the Wyrrester planet of Typholchaktas in the Furey-King Maelstrom. But they hadn't been transmat waves. The energy had been on telepathic frequencies, and the Doctor recognised the waveform.

It was almost identical to the telepathic energy that the TARDIS used.

He stood back from the console, angry with himself for not realising what had happened sooner. If he was correct then the mind that inhabited Clara's body was that of a Wyrrester, and Clara... he couldn't even begin to image what she must be going though. Assuming that the transference had been successful, that was. If it hadn't, then she might be nothing more than a disembodied telepathic wraith, doomed to drift through the Furey-King Maelstrom for ever.

Either way, there was no way that he could possibly destroy the Bell until he had reversed the process.

He glanced at the vial of purple liquid perched on the central console.

At least he had something to bargain with.

It took every ounce of Clara's willpower to stop her mind descending into pure, blind panic. Slowly she tried to slow her breathing and her heartbeat, trying to find familiar sensations in the alien body in which she was now trapped.

With huge effort she forced herself to speak.

'Where… am I?'

The second scorpion scuttled forward, its surprise plain to see, even on such an alien face. 'It can talk? You did not say that it would be able to talk!'

'They always did show signs of potential,' said the smaller one. 'Although, this one does indeed seem to be a quite remarkable example of its species.'

'Please…' Clara struggled to get her new mouth to force out the words. 'Who are you?'

The smaller creature tucked its claws across its chest. 'I am Chief Researcher Maagla. My colleague is General Legriss. Do you understand what has happened to you?'

Clara struggled to recall the events of a few moments ago. 'They put me in the centre of the circle. A voice said something about me being a vessel.'

'The voice that you heard was that of our Head Scientist, Gebbron. Through his genius he has been able to transplant his mind into your human body. You in turn now inhabit his form.'

'So I… I'm on…'

'The planet Typholchaktas. It may come a shock to you to discover that you are billions of miles from your homeworld.'

'*That's* what you think will come as a shock to me? Not being in the body of a giant scorpion?' Clara tried to laugh, but the only sound she could make was a burbling cough.

'Scorpion?' Maagla tilted his head on one side in an almost human gesture. 'I do not understand the word.'

'Never mind.'

Maagla scuttled forward, his claws touching controls on the consoles that surrounded them and Clara suddenly felt the force that held her dissipate.

'Is that wise?' snapped the other Wyrrester gruffly. 'This creature could be dangerous.'

'I do not think so,' replied Maagla. 'Besides. Where is she going to go?'

Slowly Clara tried to move the body that she found herself trapped in, staggering forward almost drunkenly. 'OK, six legs, that's tricky.'

Orientating herself, she turned in a slow circle, desperately trying not to let her gaze rest too long whenever she caught a glimpse of herself in the polished surface and glass screens of the control consoles.

She was in a laboratory of some kind. Or a hospital. The lack of anything that even remotely resembled human technology made it almost impossible to find a common frame of reference. The walls were some hard, grey stone, almost like granite. Light from hidden sources bathed everything in a sickly yellowish light. She was standing in a circle of stones, each made from the same granite-like rock as the walls, each with the same swirling patterns as the circle back on Earth.

'What is this place?'

'You are in the Bunker. That is all the information you need,' hissed the larger of the creatures.

'You must forgive General Legriss.' Maagla raised his claws apologetically. 'He has the mind of a soldier. Come, let me show you.'

Ignoring the protests of the other Wyrrester, Maagla led Clara from the laboratory, ushering her down a wide passage constructed from the same grey stone. At the end of the passageway Clara could see reddish light, and there was a sound; a bubbling, hissing, screaming roar that made her hesitate.

'What is that?'

'That is the sound of our species dying.'

They emerged onto a wide balcony. The air above them fizzed and crackled, and Clara realised that it was a force field of some kind. Maagla scuttled forward to the balcony edge. 'This is how it ends...'

Clara edged forward to join him, staring in disbelieving horror at the scene in front of her.

They stood at the top of a tall, featureless building in the remains of a shattered, ruined city. Once-proud spires now stood blackened and crumbling beneath a boiling scarlet sky. Strange alien craft lay smashed and twisted amongst the rubble, black smoke rising in huge columns filled with ash and glowing embers.

And as far as the eye could see, to the edge of the city and out to the distant mountains beyond, the landscape was crawling with Wyrresters. Millions of them, crawling over their fellows, a seething, screaming mass of insect bodies, clawing to stay on top of the pile.

It was a vision of hell.

Maagla turned to Clara and the alien visage cracked into a horrible semblance of a smile.

'Welcome to my world.'

Back on Earth, Gebbron, the Wyrrester in Clara's body, looked around the strange building in which he found himself. It never ceased to amaze him how much unnecessary clutter these creatures surrounded themselves with. Even Clearfield, brilliant as he was, still retained the untidy compulsions of the rest of his species.

He watched as one of the soldiers guided another human male into the room, leading him to a metal receptacle that stood against the wall and dousing his head with water. The acrid reek of the insecticide on his skin made Gebbron want to retch. He had heard the death cries of the insects outside as the chemical had destroyed their nervous systems, but in his mind he had felt the deaths of the Wyrresters who had been inside those bodies.

He felt a blaze of hatred for these pitiful creatures. If they had been able to complete the bridgehead seventy years earlier, none of these animals would ever had existed.

Another two of the soldiers entered the room and Gebbron took an involuntary step backwards as he saw that one of them was carrying the pressurised canister of insecticide spray.

One of the men, an obvious leader, turned to face him.

'I'm Captain Wilson, British Army. Are you able to give me any useful intel about what is going on out there?'

To Gebbron's relief the other human, the female called Angela, was more than happy to speak.

As she explained to the soldier about the laboratory and the experiments taking place at the industrial estate, Gebbron took the opportunity to weigh up the opposition that he faced. For the most part they would be relatively easy to dispose of: the man seemed old, and obviously unwell; the smaller human was nothing more than a frightened child. The female was fit, and of equal weight, so she would be a challenge, but not an impossible one. No. It was the soldiers that would prove to be the most difficult obstacle.

He scrutinised the weapons that they were carrying. They were considerably more sophisticated than the ones that had been used against his species previously. The humans had obviously made significant military advances in seventy years. Perhaps there might be a place for some of these human creatures after all in the new order.

The discussion between Angela and the soldier had become heated, and Gebbron returned his attention to what they were saying.

'Don't be ridiculous! The Doctor isn't behind this, he's doing everything he can to stop it! Clara, tell him!'

A sly thought entered Gebbron's head. If he could suggest to these soldiers that the Doctor *was* part of this, sow the seeds of dissent amongst this group, then that could only be to her advantage…

As Gebbron opened Clara's mouth to speak, the other male, the one who had been riding the bike, interrupted. 'Captain, I can vouch for the Doctor. Without him, all of us here would be either zombies or dead by now.' He turned and looked at Gebbron with a conspiratorial smile. 'I envy you, Clara, travelling with him.'

Aware that the moment for his deception had passed, Gebbron forced the body he had stolen to smile back.

'Right then.' The leader of the soldiers had obviously reached some kind of decision. 'Now that we know the location of our objective I suggest that we get on with our mission. Arnopp, Palmer, you're with me. Hawkins, you stay here with the civilians, inform the Colonel that we have a positive ID on the location of the Bell.'

'Sir!' All three soldiers snapped to attention, then two of them followed their leader out to the primitive transportation device at the front of the dwelling.

As the three men clambered aboard and the engine coughed into life, Gebbron allowed himself a smile of satisfaction. The odds had just turned significantly in his favour.

Clearfield watched as the last few insects were finally herded back into their cages, the air as thick with the smell of ozone. Cattle prods might not have been the subtlest way of getting the job done, but they were efficient.

He turned back to where technicians were swarming around the Bell, trying to repair the damage that the Doctor had done. He glanced at his watch. Less than three hours to the vernal equinox.

'Well? Have you found out what's wrong yet?' he snapped.

One of the technicians turned slowly to face him. 'A Xerum 525 fluid link has been removed.' His voice was slurred and emotionless.

Clearfield felt a jolt of panic. Xerum 525 was one of the few components that they could not replace. They had tried with limited success to synthesise an alternative. If he failed the Wyrresters…

'Start preparation of replacement solution 540.'

'Solution 540 has not been effective in full-power tests…'

'Just do it!'

'Tut, tut, tut. Getting snippy with the workforce, are we? That's never going to engender a good working environment.'

Clearfield turned to see the Doctor walking slowly across the warehouse floor towards him. Several of the technicians hurried to intercept him, but Clearfield waved them away. 'Doctor. How nice of you to give me another opportunity to kill you.' He shook his head, smiling. 'But you're too clever for that, aren't you. Let me guess. Kill you and I'll never discover where you've hidden the Xerum 525, correct?'

'Actually, it's right here.' The Doctor reached into his jacket and withdrew the glass vial.

'Then perhaps you're not as clever as I thought.' Clearfield raised his revolver. 'If you've brought it back then can you give me a good reason why I don't just shoot you right now, and take it from your dead hands.'

'Well,' said the Doctor holding up the vial in front of his face. 'That depends on whether you're colour blind or not.'

Clearfield stared at the vial in horror. The once violet liquid was now a dark green. 'What have you done?'

'Something very, *very* clever actually.' The Doctor tossed the vial into the air and caught it again. 'I've tweaked its structure slightly at a subatomic level. Quite simple to make the necessary adjustments to the control circuits so that it will still function as it should, but only if you have the right formula.' He tapped a finger to the side of his head. 'And that's in here.'

'And I'm guessing that the price for that will be the safe return of Miss Oswald's mind to her body. How very predictable.'

'The oldies are the goldies.' The Doctor held out the vial. 'So, do we have a deal?'

Clearfield nodded.

'Good!' The Doctor handed the modified Xerum 525 to one of the waiting technicians and turned to examine the insects lurking in their cages.

'Didn't really get a proper chance to look at these earlier. Very impressive! The creatures currently loose in the village are earlier, less successful experiments, I'm guessing. But these…' He peered into one of the cages. 'A synaptically enhanced hybrid of spider, ant, mosquito and crane fly. Shells for the Wyrresters to transfer their consciousness into when you turn on the machine during the equinox.'

'Excellent, Doctor.' Clearfield nodded approvingly. 'With the stone circle incomplete, a full physical transference was no longer possible, but a mental transfer… It just took some time to find the perfect hybrid of insects that was suitable for their minds to inhabit.'

'But why?' The Doctor spun to face him, his eyes narrowing. 'Why are you doing this? What have they told you?'

'Our race has no future here,' explained Maagla. 'We have long passed the point where our numbers can be sustained by the planet's resources. There are no other suitable planets in our system, we have nowhere left to go.'

'So you figured that you'd just take over the Earth?'

'We were looking for a way to save ourselves! The stone circles that exist on your planet and ours, and many others, are the remnants of technology from a long-dead race. A technology that we have worked long to understand and control. When functioning properly the circles are capable of acting as transmat stations across unimaginable distances... Seventy of your years ago we opened up a link with your planet. Sadly, that option is no longer open to us.'

'But even if it were, you can't just transport millions of your people onto Earth. The results would be catastrophic!'

'Millions of us?' Maagla gave a wicked laugh. 'We have no interest in saving the squabbling masses down there. They have already relinquished their entitlement to life. Only we, the elite, have earned the right to survive.'

Clara backed away in horror. 'You'd abandon your own people?'

'They refused to accept our solution! Here, in this city, in this very building, Gebbron had already proved that careful, selective liquidation of certain genetic groups could drastically reduce the population. If he had been able to do this on a planetary scale...'

'Genocide,' breathed Clara. 'You were advocating mass slaughter of your own people.'

'To survive! When the only other option was death for every living creature on this planet! Gebbron should have been hailed as a saviour. Instead he is hunted and reviled.

Persecuted by our so-called leaders. This facility…'

'Shut up!' The revulsion Clara felt was almost more than she could bear. The scientists, the soldiers, the creature whose body she inhabited, and whose mind had invaded her own body, were war criminals.

The Bunker was a death camp.

Chapter

Eighteen

'Asylum seekers?' The Doctor's eyes narrowed even further. 'These are Wyrresters! Savage, brutal warmongers, without any moral compunction—'

'And Gebbron has rejected that philosophy!'

The Doctor snorted. 'A peace-loving Wyrrester! Planet after planet in the Furey-King Maelstrom has been laid waste by their military machine. Whole species decimated.'

'And it has brought them to the edge of extinction. It is true that their attempt to invade seventy years ago was a military operation, but Gebbron has abandoned that strategy. He and his fellow scientists just wish to survive.'

'Man and Wyrrester living side by side in harmony?'

Clearfield glared at him. 'They are our superior in every way. They can guide man to achieve his full potential.'

'And you are quite happy to help them achieve that?'

'Once they are in power, man will begin a new golden age of scientific progress. They deserve to lead us!'

'And if you believe that then I don't need my sonic

screwdriver to tell me that you're an idiot.' The Doctor shook his head. 'It's not your fault. The venom that's in your system probably contains a suggestive agent; their version of the Scopolamine you've been using to control the villagers. You've been part of Gebbron's back-up plan from the beginning.' He sniffed. 'I suppose that you've been promised a position of power in this new world order.'

Clearfield said nothing.

The Doctor just nodded. 'I thought as much. Just another quisling.'

Clearfield stiffened. 'Think what you like, Doctor, whether you like it or not, if you want to see your companion again, then you have no choice but to help me.'

'Yes.' The Doctor smiled grimly. 'I know.'

'Very well, Private Hawkins, situation understood. But I want regular updates. And I mean regular! Over and out.'

Gebbron watched the soldier carefully as he finished making his report to his superiors. Clearfield had been clumsy in his attempts at subterfuge. There was obviously a sizeable military force nearby. The first course of action would be to neutralise that force. He needed to get word to General Legriss.

There was a sudden tugging at the cloth Clara wore around her legs. Gebbron turned to see the young human child standing next to her. He recoiled in disgust at its touch.

'What?' he snapped.

'Constable Bevan says that you're a friend of the Doctor's. That you're his assistant or something?'

'What of it?'

'Do you know where he is?' The child was obviously distressed about something. 'I really need to speak to him. It's important.'

Gebbron was about to dismiss the child, but then hesitated. If this creature had something important for the Doctor then it might be of relevance.

'Is it something that you can tell me?' He did his best to sound friendly and reassuring, trying to keep the revulsion from his voice.

'I'll show you. Come on.'

Gebbron rose and followed the child to the rear door of the building. As the child opened it and indicated to him that he should follow him, Gebbron allowed himself a smile of satisfaction. This could work out better than he had thought. A chance to dispose of this human in private.

Checking that none of the others had seen them leave, he followed the child into the enclosure at the rear of the property. Once again he found herself bemused by the humans insistence on surrounding themselves with trinkets. If they only knew how it was to share every inch of space with dozen upon dozen of your fellows…

The child was pulling at the foliage at the side of the path. Gebbron tensed. Once the child had told him what it was that he knew, his death needed to be swift, and done in such a way that it would cause maximum panic amongst the others.

He moved swiftly towards the child, then caught sight of the thing that he was struggling to uncover and stopped, barely able to believe his eyes.

The ancient symbols in the rock were unmistakable. The means of opening the portal to Gebbron's own world had been here in this place all this time.

Gebbron threw back his head and roared with exultant laughter.

After seventy years of assuming it had been destroyed, here was the missing stone from the circle.

As the vintage motorcycle and sidecar roared along the country road towards the industrial estate, Corporal Palmer, sitting in the sidecar with the two anti-tank weapons resting in front of him, turned to Captain Wilson with a grin.

'Just like *Indiana Jones and the Last Crusade*, eh, Captain?' he yelled.

Wilson, clinging tightly to the back seat of the Norton, rolled his eyes. Dobby Palmer was a real film buff. 'Personally, I always preferred *The Great Escape!*' he shouted back.

'Well, Arnopp had better not try and jump any fences in this old crate.'

Before Wilson even had a chance to reply, something huge erupted from the hedgerow alongside the road, slamming into the sidecar, and sending the bike careering off the road and crashing into the adjoining field. Thrown clear by the impact, Captain Wilson hit the ground hard, the breath knocked from him.

He staggered to his feet to see the huge, armoured shape of the beetle burst through the hedge, bearing down on where the bike lay on its side. Wilson could see Arnopp and Palmer struggling to pull themselves free.

Throwing his rifle to his shoulder, Wilson fired, the armour-piercing rounds tearing into the beetle's carapace. Screeching in pain it scuttled around to face him, giving the two men by the bike the time they needed to scramble clear.

Aware that the huge insect was now bearing down on him, Wilson started to back away, still firing in short, controlled bursts. Despite the damage he was causing, he didn't seem to be slowing the monster down. Concentrating on his target, and not on where he was putting his feet, Wilson felt his left leg give way beneath him as he stepped into a rabbit burrow.

He crashed to the ground, pain lancing up his leg as his ankle twisted awkwardly. As the creature seized its opportunity and rushed forward to strike, Captain Wilson thought about how ridiculous it was that a man was about to be squashed by a beetle.

The creature was almost on him when it stopped, screeching in alarm. As it began to back away, Wilson started to scramble to his feet. Then he became aware of a shadow falling over him, and long bristle-covered legs planting themselves on the grass either side of him.

He looked up in horror to see the vast abdomen of the spider looming over him, blotting out the sky. He froze, pressing his body flat onto the grass as the spider slunk forward, hissing angrily at the beetle that was attempting to steal its prey.

The two huge monsters circled each other warily for a moment, then, in a blur of movement, the spider struck. Wilson scrambled to get clear as the two insects smashed together, their screams echoing around the English countryside. Already weakened by the damage caused by the armour-piercing bullets, the beetle crashed to the ground, and the spider lunged forward to sink its fangs into the flesh of its head.

Gritting his teeth against the pain in his leg, Wilson hauled himself to his feet and ran. In the distance he could see Arnopp and Palmer kneeling by the wreckage of the bike and his eyes widened as he caught sight of a familiar shape being hoisted onto Arnopp's shoulder. Moments later there was the dull 'crump' of a portable anti-tank missile being fired.

Wilson threw himself forward into the grass, hands covering his head as the missile struck its target and the beetle exploded in a cloud of shell and guts. As the volatile chemicals in its abdomen mixed there was yet another explosion, and boiling acid burst out with devastating effect.

Hit by the full force of the caustic spray, the spider reeled backwards, legs flailing wildly. Within seconds it was nothing but a misshapen lump of steaming flesh hissing quietly in the long grass.

Wilson hauled himself to his feet as Arnopp and Palmer hurried over to him. Arnopp's nose wrinkled in disgust as he peered at the shattered remains of the two huge insects.

'I never did like bugs.'

'Private Hawkins, Miss Drabble, you'd better come and see this.'

Robin Sanford was peering worriedly through the curtains of his front room into the rapidly darkening afternoon light.

The others joined him, and Angela gave a gasp as she caught sight of what was approaching.

'What the hell is this?' murmured Hawkins.

It looked as though the entire village was walking towards them; men, women, children, all marching in unison down the narrow road, their faces drawn and heavy, their arms hanging limply by their sides.

Snatching up his rifle, Hawkins ran from the room. 'Stay here!'

Angela raced after him. 'Private Hawkins, wait!'

She caught up with the private outside the house. He had his rifle to his shoulder, covering the zombie-like villagers as they filed silently into the yard. Angela could see faces she recognised: Simon George, Emily Nichols, even Gabby, still clutching her son to her chest.

'You can't just open fire on these people! You can't!'

'Yeah, well you and I know that, but maybe they don't.'

He lifted the barrel of the assault rifle and Angela covered her ears as he fired a quick burst over the heads of the oncoming crowd.

'I want everyone to stop where they are! Right now!'

To Angela's relief the crowd shambled to a halt.

'All right.' Hawkins was breathing hard. 'That's good. Now, which one of you is going to tell me what the hell this is all about?'

'Private…' Robin's trembling voice rang out from the doorway. 'I think that you might be looking in the wrong direction for that.'

Hawkins and Angela spun. Robin was standing in the doorway, but it was Clara that captured their attention. Eyes wild with an animal intensity, she was gripping Kevin Alperton by the nape of the neck, practically lifting the boy off his feet.

'Clara?' Angela started to move towards her. 'What on earth…?'

'Stand still!' Clara spat the words. 'Take another step and the human child will die.'

'The human child?' Hawkins swung his rifle around, uncertain whether to keep it trained on the eerily silent crowd or the situation unfolding behind him. 'What the hell does she mean?'

Angela stared at her sadly, suddenly knowing what had happened to her friend in the circle. 'But you're not Clara, are you? Not on the inside. You're one of them.'

'Exactly!' She squeezed Kevin's neck, making him cry out in pain. 'Now put the weapon down!'

With no other option open to him, Private Hawkins did as he was told. Immediately the crowd surged forward, grasping him and Angela by the arms.

'Who are you?' asked Angela, struggling to break free from the grip of people that she had once called her friends. 'What is it that you want?'

'I am Gebbron, Chief Scientist of the Wyrrester Scientific Corps.' The thing controlling Clara's body gave a horrible smile. 'And you will soon learn to love me as your leader.'

Chapter

Nineteen

With his leg strapped up, and a shot of painkillers from Corporal Palmer's medical pouch, Captain Wilson managed to struggle back onto his feet. The Norton was a write-off, and Palmer's sniper rifle was bent and twisted beyond repair, but they still had one of the NLAWs left, and more than enough grenades to make quite a mess of the Bell when they found it.

That was assuming there were no more giant insects lying in wait for them en route...

He glanced at his army-issue Cabot watch. The two hours that they had been given were almost up. He just hoped that Hawkins had been able to convince the Colonel to give them more time.

They were about to set off towards the industrial estate when Private Arnopp suddenly paused. 'Listen,' he hissed.

From somewhere ahead of them came the sound of a large crowd of people moving along one of the lanes. Wilson motioned to the two soldiers to move forward and the three men made their way quickly to the hedgerow at the edge of the field and peered cautiously into the road.

'Looks like a goddamn town meeting,' breathed Palmer.

Wilson recognised the quote from *Aliens* but ignored it. Palmer was right. If the research that they had about the population of Ringstone was correct then it was pretty much all of them, and they seemed to be carrying something.

He twisted to get a better view; it seemed to be a large, heavy stone of some kind. Then he caught sight of something that made him curse under his breath. At the front of the crowd, being marched along with his own rifle pointed at his back, was Private Hawkins. Robin Sanford, the constable, and the other civilians walked alongside him.

Wilson quickly considered his options. They still had to get to the Bell, but he couldn't just abandon one of his men. Besides, they needed Hawkins to get back in touch with the Colonel if they were going to cancel that airstrike.

'Dobby, follow them. If you get a chance to get Hawkins and the others free, take it. Arnopp, you're with me.'

Both men nodded and Palmer started to make his way along the hedgerow.

'Palmer.'

The corporal turned to look at his commanding officer. 'Yes, Captain?'

'Remember that these are civilians, Palmer. We don't want a bloodbath here.'

Palmer nodded and hurried away.

Private Arnopp gave Wilson a worried look. 'And then there were two…'

Shirtsleeves rolled up, the Doctor was arm-deep inside the Bell, helping to repair the mounting point for the Xerum 525 vial when one of the villagers entered the warehouse and shambled towards Clearfield.

'Gebbron wishes you to join him at the circle.'

'I'm busy,' snapped the professor concentrating on the console in front of him.

'He says that that it is important. That I am to use force if you will not come.'

'Better do as he says,' said the Doctor in a cautioning tone. 'I don't know about Gebbron, but Clara can be quite forceful when she wants to be. A real bossy-boots.'

Throwing his clipboard down in disgust, Clearfield glared at him, then turned and hurried out through the doors.

As soon as Clearfield was out of sight, the Doctor clambered to his feet, rolling down his sleeves and shrugging back into his jacket. He needed to work fast.

'Right, you lot.' He clicked his fingers at the other technicians. 'I imagine that there's enough Scopolamine in your systems to make this relatively simple.' He pressed his fingers this temples, his brow furrowing with concentration. 'You will carry on with your allotted tasks, you will ignore me and anything I do. Indicate your understanding.'

As one, the shambling technicians nodded.

The Doctor allowed himself a smile of satisfaction. 'It's all a matter of willpower...'

He crossed to the far side of the warehouse, searching through the piles of electrical components until he found a coil of thick, insulated cable.

'That should do the job,' he muttered to himself.

Dragging the heavy cable across the floor, he started to uncoil it. Leaving one end next to the Bell he pushed open one of the fire escape doors and hauled the other end of the cable across to where the TARDIS stood outside.

Opening the door, he vanished inside, hauling the cable over to the console and connecting it as best he could. When it was done, he stood back and grimaced. It was a bit of a lash-up, but he needed access to both the dematerialisation and telepathic circuits if this was going to work properly.

He hurried back into the warehouse, busying himself with the connections at the other end. He was making the last connection to the Bell when there was the sharp click of a safety catch being unlocked and the cold barrel of a gun pressed into the back of his neck.

'OK, hands where I can see them. Quickly.'

The Doctor pressed his hands onto the surface of the Bell. Rough hands quickly patted him down and he was spun around. Two bruised and bloodied British soldiers faced him, guns raised.

The Doctor gave a gasp of exasperation. 'Why is it I can always rely on the armed forces to arrive at *precisely* the wrong moment?'

The first soldier grinned, but didn't take his finger from the trigger. 'And there I was thinking that we were like the American Cavalry, arriving to save the day just in the nick of time.'

The Doctor glanced at the rank on his sleeve. 'Captain, if you are interested in saving the day, then you really need to let me finish what I am doing, I have a very complex set of calculations to make and very little time in which to do it.'

The soldier hesitated for a moment, then lowered the rifle. 'The Doctor, right?'

'Yes!'

'I'm Captain Wilson, this is Private Arnopp…'

'Yes, yes, yes. Introductions later, Captain.' The Doctor turned back to his work. 'Clearfield could be back any moment.'

'Clearfield?' Wilson frowned, remembering the classified documents that Colonel Dickinson had shown him. 'There was a Professor Clearfield in charge of the experiments during the war.'

'Yes.' The Doctor didn't turn around. 'And he's very close to successfully starting up them up again. Now, if you don't mind…'

Wilson walked slowly around the huge grey shape that dominated the warehouse. 'So this is the Bell…'

'If you want to be completely accurate, this is *Die Glocke*,' said the Doctor without looking up. 'German engineering. Always a pleasure to work with.'

Wilson glanced at Arnopp. 'What do you think, Private?'

Arnopp made a swift assessment of the machine. 'Outside looks ceramic. Steel core. Shouldn't be a problem, Captain. We should have enough grenades to turn it into scrap.'

The Doctor raised his head, his brow furrowed. 'Now you just listen here, Captain. If you think for one moment—'

'No, you listen to me, Doctor. I have strict instructions to disable or destroy this machine in any way possible. Now unless you can give me a damn good reason—'

'Clara Oswald.'

'I'm sorry?'

'You asked me for a good reason. She's it. Clara Oswald.'

Wilson frowned. 'The girl we left back at the farm?'

The Doctor shook his head. 'Whatever it is that you have met, it is not Clara, just a thing inhabiting her body.' The Doctor leaned close to the captain, his voice low. 'Do you have family, Captain Wilson, someone close to you? Well, imagine if one of them was trapped, trapped somewhere terrible, and frightening, and more alien than you could possibly imagine. Wouldn't you do anything to help them? Wouldn't you take whatever risks you could in order to bring them back safely? Well, that is what I am asking. Clara is trapped, in a strange body, on a strange world. This machine can bring her back. Give me the chance to save her.'

Wilson was silent for a moment. 'I have a niece,' he said finally. 'My sister's kid. Diagnosed with leukaemia last year. If I could do anything that could help her...' He looked at the Doctor sadly. 'But I can't. And neither can you. If this machine activates, then my commanding officer has orders to bring in an airstrike that will leave this entire village as nothing more than a smoky hole in the ground.'

The Doctor stared at him in horror. 'Then stop it.'

'Not my decision.'

'Captain!' The Doctor's voice was like a thunderclap. 'I need this machine to operate for a fraction of a second in order to get Clara back. After that, I will happily turn it into so much molten slag. But I *will* have that fraction of a second!'

The two men faced each other for what seemed like an age, then Wilson nodded. 'All right, Doctor. But as soon as your friend is safe, we destroy this machine.'

'My word,' said the Doctor solemnly. 'Now, the two of you need to get out of here before Clearfield comes back.'

Wilson checked his watch. 'I'm assuming all this is going to kick off in about fifteen minutes. At the equinox?'

The Doctor looked at him with surprise and nodded. 'You've done your research, Captain.'

The sound of booted feet approaching made the

Captain look up sharply, hand reaching for his weapon. A third soldier hurried into the warehouse.

Wilson relaxed his grip. 'You're going to be the death of me, Corporal Palmer. Sneaking in like that.'

'Sorry, sir.' Palmer grinned.

'So, what's the news?'

'Private Hawkins and the others are being held on the edge of a field on the other side of the railway. Couple of the zombies have got Hawkins' rifle and Mr Sanford's shotgun. The villagers are still doing their Wicker Man bit. That young bird? She got them putting a stone into the circle.'

'A stone?' The Doctor was on his feet in a flash. 'What stone? Corporal, I need you to tell me exactly what is going on out there, and quickly!'

Clearfield stepped into the stone circle, staring with incredulity at the stone that the villagers were placing into position.

'I don't believe it…' he said weakly, running his hand over the ancient rock. 'It was here... All this time…'

'You are an idiot, Clearfield!' Clara, or rather Gebbron, was almost purple with anger. 'Years wasted! Endless pointless experiments!'

'But, where…?'

'Right under your nose! In the house of this man.'

Gebbron pointed at where Robin Sanford was held alongside Angela and the others.

Almost in a daze, Clearfield walked towards him.

'You took this? You kept this hidden. Why?' His voice hardened with anger. 'Why?'

Robin stared at him defiantly. 'Because I knew that if I didn't then one day someone would come back. To reopen the gateway. To bring back the monsters.' He shook his head. 'I'd seen it happen once. I wasn't going to let it happen again. Figured that even if you could build another one of those damn machines you wouldn't be able to just replace one of the stones.'

Clearfield leaned close, recognition dawning on him. 'You were there, weren't you? One of the soldiers…' He studied him carefully. 'Age has not been kind to you.'

Robin sniffed. 'Still got all my face, though, haven't I?'

Clearfield's rage and frustration boiled up. He was about to strike the old man when Clara's voice barked out across the circle.

'We've no time for this, Clearfield!'

He took a deep, shuddering breath and turned away from Robin Sanford. 'No, Gebbron.'

He hurried over to where she was examining the stone. 'Is it damaged in any way?' he asked, peering at the swirling patterns.

'No. It has been well treated.' Gebbron flashed an unpleasant smile at Robin. 'You should have destroyed it when you had the chance.' He turned back to Clearfield. 'Contact Maagla. Tell him that our plans have changed. He is to get my physical form ready for immediate transfer to this planet.' Gebbron looked down at his human form. 'I loathe this abomination of a body. You will operate the

Bell so that my consciousness is reunified the instant that it materialises. And tell General Legriss to prepare his guards.'

Clearfield just nodded, aware that all his plans all his preparations had been for nothing. 'What about the girl? You wish her reunified as well?'

Gebbron said nothing.

'Gebbron, if we do not transfer her mind at the same moment then it will have nowhere to go! It will just dissipate.'

'Then so be it.'

The Doctor had only just finished connecting the Bell to his TARDIS when Clearfield re-entered the laboratory.

'Something wrong?'

Clearfield looked at him blankly. The scientist looked older, frailer, suddenly. 'We must reset the machine to the 1944 calibrations. All this –' he waved a hand at the circle of black monoliths – 'wasted.'

The Doctor watched the man carefully as he stepped forward to one of the control consoles and started readjusting controls to their new settings. He was on the edge of a breakdown, of total collapse. If ever there was a chance to break through the Wyrrester conditioning…

'Clearfield. If you do this, if you open that gateway, then there will be no stopping them.'

Clearfield looked at him blankly. 'What?'

'If you give the Wyrresters asylum here on Earth then they will destroy this world, as they have destroyed every other world they have landed on.'

'No.' Clearfield shook his head. 'No, you're wrong. They will lead us to glory.'

'Listen to me—'

'It's too late, Doctor.' Clearfield snatched the gun from his jacket. 'Now continue setting the calibrations. I must contact Maagla.'

The Doctor watched him make his way to the communications console. 'Together, you and I might have stopped this,' he murmured sadly. 'Now I have no choice.'

Angela watched as the preparations at the circle became more animated as the sky started to darken. Some of the villagers had forcibly wrenched the concrete bollard from its footing in the circle and replaced it with the stone from Robin Sanford's garden, others had been set to task clearing the web from the underpass that led to the industrial estate.

'I wonder what's happened to the spider?' she muttered to Private Hawkins.

'With luck the Captain put paid to that,' said Hawkins firmly.

'That bang we heard earlier?'

Hawkins nodded. 'Anti-tank missile by the sound of it.'

Charlie Bevan was more concerned with what the other villagers were up to. Groups of them were dragging arm-thick cables through the cleared underpass. Cables that obviously led back towards the industrial estate. 'What are they doing?'

'Linking the circle to the Bell,' said Robin. 'It's like that night in 1944 all over again.' The thought of it was obviously terrifying him.

'But the others, the Captain and the other soldiers. They'll be able to stop it, won't they? I mean the weapons you have today...'

Hawkins said nothing, just stared at his boots. 'Look there's something you should know...'

'They're not going to let this thing go the distance, are they, son?' said Robin Sanford softly. 'They've got other plans.'

'Who?' Now it was Charlie's turn to look frightened. 'Who has other plans?'

'Our mission was to stop the Bell being activated... Or...'

'Or what?'

'Or get everyone away before the air strike.'

Robin gave a soft laugh. 'Well isn't that just perfect. I survive a bomb attack during the war and end up getting killed by one seventy years later.'

'But we've got to warn everyone!' Charlie Bevan stepped forward to try and reason with his captors, but Simon George just shoved him back roughly.

'Simon, you have to listen to me. We're all in terrible danger.'

The postmaster's expression remained unchanged.

'They can't hear you, Charlie,' said Angela wearily. 'Or

don't want to hear you.'

'But everyone is going to be killed!'

'If that maniac lets that monster loose again then everyone is dead anyway,' Robin pointed out.

Before anyone could say any more, a distant voice yelled, 'Hawkins! Fire in the hole!'

Angela pointed to the middle of the field, as several metal canisters suddenly arced over the hedge.

Hawkins' eyes went wide as he recognised the objects. 'Everyone! Close your eyes, hands over your ears. Now!'

Angela barely managed to do as she was told before the flash-bangs went off. Even with her ears blocked, the detonation was deafening, and the flash was bright enough to light up the insides of her eyelids. She opened her eyes to see villagers staggering around blindly, completely disorientated by the explosion. Two more canisters landed on the grass, but this time dense white smoke started to billow out, turning the crowd into a coughing, shambling mass of silhouetted shapes.

She suddenly felt the bonds behind her back being untied and the voice of Corporal Palmer hissing in her ear. 'Link hands, stay low, follow me.'

Struggling not to cough from the acrid smoke, Angela did as she was told, following the corporal into the trees and out into the car park beyond,

Hurrying them towards the pub, Palmer led them into the lounge bar, where they all collapsed, grateful to be free of both their bonds and the choking smoke.

Moments later Captain Wilson joined them, breathless

and sweating from his recent exertions.

'Right, that's given us a breathing space, but we don't have long.' He crossed to where Charlie Bevan was struggling to get his breath. 'Constable. We've just come from the Doctor. He said that you are to tell us how you and he survived that night.'

'What?' Charlie looked at him in bemusement. 'I'm more concerned with surviving today.'

'Listen to me,' snapped Captain Wilson hauling him to his feet. 'I've been attacked by an acid-spitting beetle, nearly trodden on by a huge spider, I've got an imminent alien invasion, not to mention a commanding officer who is probably tearing his hair out by now – and that's if he hasn't already called in a missile strike that will leave this place as a big black stain on the landscape. I have only one anti-tank missile left, and very little time, so, if you have something that is going to be of use to me I want to hear about it right now!'

'But I don't know anything!' protested the spluttering policeman.

'He said that you were lucky to survive that night, what did he mean?'

'We only just got away in time.' Charlie was struggling to remember the details of that terrifying night. 'There was the Bell, and the scorpion in the circle, and the bombing raid—'

He stopped, suddenly aware of what it was that the Doctor wanted him to tell the Captain.

'The bombing raid… We only got back to his TARDIS

that night because one of the bombs didn't go off! Captain, there's an unexploded German bomb buried right underneath the stone circle!'

Chapter

Twenty

Clara watched with concern as the Bunker became a hive of activity. Maagla had received a message of some kind, and whatever it was that he had been told, it had changed everything.

General Legriss had summoned several Wyrresters to the control area, huge creatures that were larger than their fellows, and had far more armour. She glanced at the razor edges on their huge claws. This was obviously a soldier class of some kind. It was starting to look suspiciously like an invasion force.

She looked up as Maagla entered the control room once more, his claws clacking nervously. 'What is going on, Maagla?'

'A remarkable turn of events.'

Gripping one of her claws with his own, he led her back towards the stones once more. 'It seems that Gebbron has managed to secure the means to open the bridgehead once more. Now we have a very short time in which to make ready for physical transfer.'

'Physical transfer?' Clara felt a sure of hope. 'You mean that you're going to return me to my own body?'

'We are preparing the machinery now. Gebbron wishes transfer to take place the instant that the equinox is reached. In a short time –' Maagla gave a leering smile – 'you will be free of us.'

As Chief Researcher Maagla scuttled away and started busying himself amongst the control consoles, Clara watched him suspiciously. Something about the manner of the little Wyrrester was making her feel very, very uncomfortable.

A huge readout display – its script undecipherable and alien, but its meaning all too clear – started to count down on one wall of the control room. Clara could do nothing but stand in the centre of the transmat circle and watch. Whatever was going to happen to her, she didn't think that she was going to have long to wait.

Private Hawkins hoisted the NLAW onto his shoulder, squinting through the sight and lining up the crosshairs on the stone circle.

Finding a position with a clear line of sight to the position where Charlie Bevan recalled that the unexploded bomb was lodged had proved tricky. The attic room of the pub gave him an elevated view of the circle, but it meant that he had to fire through the trees that bordered the car park. There was a gap, but it was going to be tight.

He took a deep breath, finding a good position to rest

his elbows, and accustoming himself to the weight of the missile launcher. It was bulky and squat, compared to his L115A3 rifle, and nearly double the weight. Plus he only had one chance at this. If he missed…

'Nothing like a bit of pressure.'

Clearing his head, he pressed his eye socket to the viewfinder, grateful for the night vision in the rapidly fading daylight and clearing smoke. To his relief, the crowds of villagers were starting to retreat from the circle, leaving a solitary figure in the centre of the stones.

Standing right on top of the target.

Clearfield's eyes were fixed on the clock on the wall of the laboratory, his hand poised over the controls.

The clock hit 16.50.

'Phase one power, now.' He threw a switch, and the Bell started to glow with purple light

The Doctor operated his own control, but one eye was firmly fixed on the readout on his sonic screwdriver. If he didn't get this timing absolutely right…

Clearfield shot the Doctor a stern look. 'If you're going to help your companion, then you need to make those adjustments to the Xerum 525 controls before we reach full power.'

The Doctor nodded. He was about to give up his only bargaining chip, the only thing that was keeping Clearfield from disposing of him. He was gambling on Clearfield being too busy with the operation of the Bell to take action immediately, but once the Wyrresters were through, his life expectancy was liable to be very short indeed.

He began making the necessary adjustments, his hands moving in a blur over the controls as he made complex adjustments to counter for the modifications that he had made to the vial of Xerum 525.

Clearfield watched him suspiciously for a moment, then turned his attention back to his own equipment. 'Prepare to engage phase two power.'

'Colonel? We're getting positive readings again, sir.'

Colonel Dickinson hurried over to the workstation where the technician was monitoring transmissions from the village.

'The same as before?'

'Yes, sir. But much stronger. Levels are building fast.'

'Damn.' The colonel glanced at his watch. 'Has there been any word from Captain Wilson and his team?'

A radio operator shook his head. 'No, sir, the last transmission that we had was from Private Hawkins about half an hour ago.'

'Thank you, Private.' The Colonel straightened. He had gambled, and it hadn't paid off. Now he had to act quickly. 'Signal all squad leaders. Tell them to pull everyone back, evacuate to the safe zone. The rest of you, stand down, get to your vehicles.'

As the men around him shut down their equipment and made their way out of the command vehicle, Colonel Dickinson sat back down at his desk and reached for the phone. 'This is Colonel Paddy Dickinson. We have positive confirmation of the operation of a Bell. Tell the helicopter to commence its attack run.'

The Doctor finished his adjustments and nodded grimly at Clearfield. 'You can go to full power.'

The scientist's masked face gave no hint of expression as he pushed home the final lever.

A harsh, blaring klaxon rang out around the Wyrrester bunker. At once there was a blaze of light from the circle of stones and fingers of purple energy started to arc and flicker around the walls.

As the energy levels increased, Clara began to feel a strange tugging sensation at her skin, faint at first, but building and building.

Then, suddenly there was a blaze of light, and the room around dissolved into nothingness.

Captain Wilson watched in awe as the centre of the stone circle erupted into a ball of blazing light and cracking energy. The noise was incredible, a deep, tolling chime that reverberated through the ground, practically ratting the teeth from his skull. He could hear the sound of breaking glass as a dozen or more windows in the pub shattered.

As the glow faded Wilson could see a huge dark shape hunkered down between the stones. Slowly it started to draw itself up to its full, terrifying height.

From somewhere in the distance he could hear the low 'whub-whub-whub' of helicopter rotors echoing across the countryside.

Wilson held his breath. They probably had no more than a minute before the Apache launched its payload. 'Come on, Hawkins,' he breathed. 'Come on.'

The instant that Clearfield threw the final lever the Doctor activated his sonic screwdriver, sending a series of pre-programmed instructions to the TARDIS console.

The monoliths in the centre of the laboratory flared into life, their screens dancing with swirling alien patterns. The centre of the circle became a brilliant ball of energy, lightning arcing from the metal walkways as it coalesced into a familiar shape.

The Doctor leapt from his control console, racing into the circle as Clara fully materialised, only just catching her as her legs gave out from under her.

Hoisting her into his arms, he staggered clear of the circle, placing her gently on the floor.

'Doctor?' Her eyes fluttered open. 'That is *really* not a nice way to travel.'

He grinned at her in relief. 'Nothing that a few aspirin and day on the beach at Bognor Regis won't sort out.'

'Sounds great.' She smiled weakly. 'When do we go?'

'Just a few things to sort out here first. Saving the planet, mainly.' He dived back over to the control console, hands dancing across the controls. 'Now, if I can just reverse the polarity of the Xerum flow…'

Strong hands suddenly gripped him by the shoulders, wrenching him back from the console.

'What are you doing?' screamed Clearfield. 'If you change those settings whilst the portal is open…'

The Doctor struggled to break free. 'Don't be an idiot, man! If you let the Wyrresters establish a bridgehead here then it's not just this planet that's in danger, it's the whole of the Mutters Spiral!'

Clearfield wasn't listening. He stretched out scrabbling at the controls, desperate to undo the work that the Doctor had done. The Doctor hauled him away, crashing painfully into one of the monoliths as he did so. The two men grappled on the edge of the circle.

'I will not have spent my entire life working for nothing!' screamed Clearfield, his voice hoarse.

The screech of the Bell was now deafening as it got ready to open the portal once more.

The burst of light in the centre of the circle had caught Hawkins by surprise, momentarily blinding him. Cursing, he rubbed at his right eye, brushing away the tears and peering through the sight one more.

The girl had gone, and the creature that had replaced her was truly a thing of nightmares. Hawkins steadied his breathing, keeping the crosshairs firmly sighted on the ground beneath the monster's feet.

'They'd better be right about this.'

He pressed the trigger.

*

Captain Wilson heard the anti-tank missile fire and hauled Angela and Kevin to the floor of the bar as the smoke trail streaked away through the trees.

The explosion was colossal. Detonated by the missile, the 200-pound German bomb blew the circle to smithereens. Caught by the full force of the blast, the Wyrrester was torn to pieces, its carapace shattering, legs and claws ripped from its body as earth and rock were sent spiralling into the air.

As the fireball rolled lazily into the evening sky, Wilson just hoped that Colonel Dickinson was watching.

Even though it was on the other side of the railway, the explosion rocked the laboratory, rattling the doors and windows. The energy feedback was even more catastrophic, sparks erupted from the consoles as the light from the Bell started to flicker.

Clearfield looked up in horror. 'No!' he cried. '*No!*'

The Doctor seized his moment, and tore himself free of the scientist's grip.

Off balance, Clearfield stumbled backwards, stepping across the threshold of the circle at the very moment that the Doctor slammed the controls into reverse.

There was a roar of energy as the teleport activated for the final time, and then everything was plunged into darkness as the machine shut down.

As the huge fireball rose above the trees, Colonel Dickinson turned to a technician. 'The energy readings!

Quickly, man, are they still rising?'

'No, sir. Falling rapidly. Practically at zero!'

'Private, get hold of that helicopter,' the colonel yelled at his radio operator. 'Tell them to abort!'

The private scrabbled at the controls. 'Army Air 6579. This is command HQ. Abort! Abort! Abort!'

The colonel held his breath as the insect-like shape of the Apache swooped low over the trees towards Ringstone. He could see the slim shapes of the two missiles slung on either side of the fuselage. Had the abort order come too late?

At the last moment the helicopter turned abruptly, sweeping over the treetops and arcing away from the village, its missiles unfired.

Colonel Dickinson watched it hovering in the evening sky for a moment, then closed his eyes and offered a heartfelt prayer of thanks.

It was over.

Chapter
Twenty-One

Captain Wilson opened the door to Ringstone village hall and followed Colonel Dickinson inside. All around them, the inhabitants of the village were being treated by a team of army medics.

Wilson spotted Corporal Palmer amongst the crowds, talking with Kevin Alperton. The two men made their way through the bustle towards him. Wilson smiled to himself as he caught a snatch of their conversation. The pair had been bonding over their love of horror films.

'OK, *The Wolf Man*. Original 1941 Universal version, or 2010 remake?'

'Are you serious?' Kevin Alperton gave Palmer an unbelieving look. 'Universal every time!'

'Agreed.' Palmer grinned. 'Well, what about the *Clash of the Titans* remake? Better than the 1970s film?'

Kevin thought for a moment. 'Well the original *is* a Ray Harryhausen movie...' He shook his head. 'But, it's got that stupid clockwork owl in it. Plus, I think the scorpions are more realistic in the remake.'

'Well, we'd know, wouldn't we, kid?'

'Corporal…'

Palmer jumped to attention as he spotted the two officers. 'Sir!'

'At ease, Corporal.' Colonel Dickinson glanced around the village hall. 'How are these people doing?'

'Pretty good. High levels of Scopolamine in the bloodstream is the main issue. It'll take some time for the drug to clear their systems completely, but they'll all make a full recovery. Other than that, there are a few cuts and bruises from the explosion, a couple of mild concussions and one broken wrist.'

Dickinson nodded in approval. All three men knew that it could have been an awful lot worse. 'The Scopolamine…' he said thoughtfully. 'It can induce short-term memory loss, yes?'

'Yes, sir.'

'Well, that might be a blessing in the long run. Could save an awful lot of awkward questions.' He sighed. 'Well, I've got to debrief the Secretary of State for Defence. I'll leave you to clear up matters here, Captain Wilson.'

Wilson saluted smartly. 'Sir.'

Colonel Dickinson returned the salute, then gave Wilson a warm smile. 'Thank you, Captain. You saved a lot of lives today. I'm very grateful to you.' Pulling on his cap, he turned and pushed his way through the crowd to the open door.

Captain Wilson watched as Dickinson was led off to a car waiting on the village green. As the car pulled away there was the roar of a diesel engine and a truck pulled into the village. They had been coming and going all night, taking away the charred and broken pieces of the Wyrrester's body, removing the hybrid insects and machinery from the industrial estate. Everything was being bundled into unmarked crates and spirited away by black-uniformed special ops soldiers. Wilson wasn't happy about it one bit, and neither was the colonel, but their orders were clear. Cooperate, or be relieved of duty. Clearfield's records had noted the number of giant insects that had been released into the village, and as far as they could tell all of them had been destroyed except for one of the mosquitoes. Wilson's team had been tasked with tracking it down.

'Any idea where they're taking everything, sir?' asked Palmer, following Wilson's gaze.

'I've been told not to ask that question, Corporal,' said Wilson grimly. 'Department C-19 are in charge, and apparently that's all the information that we need to know.'

'It's probably just like the end of *Raiders of the Lost Ark*,' piped up Kevin. 'There'll be a big warehouse somewhere, where they'll lock everything away, and we'll never hear of any of this again.'

Wilson nodded. If that truly were the case, if the world never heard of the Bell again, then that would suit him just fine.

Angela stood with Clara, Robin Sanford and Charlie

Bevan in the meadow on the outskirts of Ringstone, watching as the Doctor unlocked the doors of his police box. He had moved it here as soon as the soldiers had started arriving, muttering something about 'never forgiving Winston Churchill for offering that reward'.

Angela didn't know whether to take him seriously or not. She turned to look at Clara. The young woman looked very pale and very tired. 'Are you OK?'

'Me? Oh, yeah. I'm fine.' Clara smiled

'But that thing… It really did take over your body, didn't it?'

'All in a day's work.' She tried her best to keep her voice light, but her smile faded at the memory.

Angela held her gaze. 'The thing is, you really mean that, don't you?'

Clara gave her a hug. 'Trust me. I'll be fine.'

'Right, we should be on our way.' The Doctor glared at army trucks and soldiers swarming through the village. 'Getting too busy around here for my liking.'

'Do you think they'll try and repair the Bell?' asked Robin anxiously. 'Try and start up the experiments again?'

'Well, they're stupid enough to try,' said the Doctor witheringly. 'So, just in case, I've done enough damage to the machinery to keep them busy repairing it for decades.'

'And what about Clearfield?' asked Charlie. 'What will have happened to him?'

'I really don't know,' said the Doctor quietly. 'He stepped into the influence of the techno-circle at the exact moment that it went into reverse phase. His body was either totally dismembered at an atomic level by the teleport beam, or…'

'Or he's on Typholchaktas?' Clara starred at him in horror.

The Doctor nodded. 'He finally gets to see his alien world.'

Clara shuddered. A single human being alone on a planet of billions of Wyrresters. Even after all that the scientist had done, she wouldn't wish that fate on anyone.

The five of them stood in silence for a moment, but then the clatter of an army helicopter whirling through the night sky spurred the Doctor into action.

Grabbing hold of Clara's hand, he hurried her over towards the TARDIS and pushed her inside. Clara managed to shout a hurried series of goodbyes before the doors slammed shut and the light on top of the police box started to flash steadily.

Angela watched in amazement as, with a swirl of wind and a grating, asthmatic roar, the police box vanished from view.

'Well, I'll be damned…' Robin Sanford stared open-mouthed at the patch of grass where the box had just been. 'I *knew* that I'd heard a wheezing groaning noise that night!'

With a laugh, Angela linked one arm with him and the other with Charlie, and led the two men back towards the village.

Epilogue

Józef Razowski gave a sigh of relief as the soldier finally waved his truck forwards, and he swung onto the A303 and moving traffic at last.

He had been stuck in almost stationary queues for most of the day; every road that he had tried to turn down was either blocked off or choked with vehicles. With the radio seemingly dead, there had been no way of finding out what was going on, and the soldiers that he had tried to engage with had been unable to tell him anything other than there had been 'an incident'.

He snorted. An incident. That could mean just about anything. It was the same in Poland; the authorities would never give you a straight answer.

He pressed his foot onto the accelerator, desperate to make up for the time that he had lost, and the radio that had been unhelpfully dead all day suddenly blared back into life. As he reached forward, fumbling with the controls to try and reduce the volume, something hit the windscreen of the van with a load 'thump'.

The impact made him jump and he grasped the steering wheel with both hands once more as the van lurched across the carriageway.

The windshield was covered in thick yellow goo, legs and pieces of wing splashed everywhere. The bug must have been enormous; he could barely see out.

Cursing under his breath, he reached for the windscreen washer, and, as the wipers stared to clean the remains of the huge insect from the glass, he finally managed to find a radio channel with music, and settled into his seat for the long drive ahead.

Acknowledgements

Huge thanks to Justin Richards and Albert DePetrillo, for inviting me to be part of a whole new regeneration cycle.

To Sue Cowley, for weaving my own personal web.

To Ian Furey-King at www.ackacklivinghistory.org. uk for invaluable information about Second World War searchlights.

To Polly and Beans, and their pet Steve, for hospitality and support.

To Steve Cole for encouragement.

To Nick, Rocky, Colin, Paul, Pete, Peter and Spike, for getting me that second bookend.

To Lee Binding, for superb attention to detail.

To the cast and crew of *Doctor Who*, with special thanks to Marcus Wilson.

To Moogie and Baz.

And, most importantly, to Karen, for saying 'Yes'.

B B C
DOCTOR WHO
Silhouette

JUSTIN RICHARDS

ISBN 978-0-8041-4088-1

'Vastra and Strax and Jenny? Oh no, we don't need to bother them. Trust me.'

Marlowe Hapworth is found dead in his locked study, killed by an unknown assailant. This is a case for the Great Detective, Madame Vastra.

Rick Bellamy, bare-knuckle boxer, has the life drawn out of him by a figure dressed as an undertaker. This angers Strax the Sontaran.

The Carnival of Curiosities, a collection of bizarre and fascinating sideshows and performers. This is where Jenny Flint looks for answers.

How are these things connected? And what does Orestes Milton, rich industrialist, have to do with it all? As the Doctor and Clara join the hunt for the truth, they find themselves thrust into a world where nothing and no one are what they seem.

An original novel featuring the Twelfth Doctor and Clara, as played by Peter Capaldi and Jenna Coleman